"My Little Lucy," He Murmured.

"I want to make love to you. I was going to give you time, but now—

Jonathan moved in before Lucy was even aware that he had changed his position. She felt his hand on her shoulder and turned around to face him. His head blotted out her view of the camels and the Colossi, and the longing for his touch washed through her, leaving her weak with desire.

His kiss was possessive and expert. Taking advantage of her indecision, he gathered her closer, once more to taste the sweetness of her response with a thoroughness that left no doubt as to his intentions.

"My little Lucy," he murmured.

ELIZABETH HUNTER
uses the world as her backdrop. She paints with broad and colorful strokes, yet she is meticulous in her eye for detail. Well-known for her warm understanding of her characters, she is internationally beloved by her loyal and enthusiastic readers.

Dear Reader:

I'd like to take this opportunity to thank you for all your support and encouragement of Silhouette Romances.

Many of you write in regularly, telling us what you like best about Silhouette, which authors are your favorites. This is a tremendous help to us as we strive to publish the best contemporary romances possible.

All the romances from Silhouette Books are for you, so enjoy this book and the many stories to come.

Karen Solem
Editor-in-Chief
Silhouette Books

ELIZABETH HUNTER
Legend of the Sun

Silhouette *Romance*

Published by Silhouette Books New York

America's Publisher of Contemporary Romance

SILHOUETTE BOOKS
300 E. 42nd St., New York, N.Y. 10017

Distributed by Pocket Books

ISBN: 0-373-08360-2

First Silhouette Books printing May, 1985

10 9 8 7 6 5 4 3 2 1

Map by Ray Lundgren

America's Publisher of Contemporary Romance

Printed in the U.S.A.

Books by Elizabeth Hunter

Silhouette Romance

For Mrs. Gigi Ghanem, with love.
And in memory of Umm Seti,
who preferred detective stories,
but would have put up with anything
to do with her beloved Egypt.

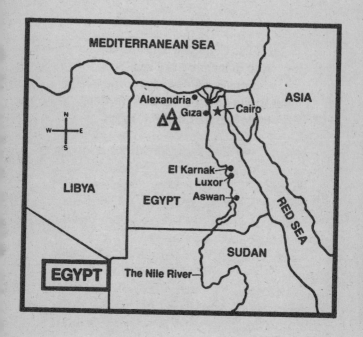

Chapter One

The felucca came slowly towards her, its dramatic single sail filling with the light breeze as it pointed upwards to the cloudless blue sky. Lucy waved an idle hand to the two men on board and was rewarded by an enthusiastic leaping up and down that almost overturned the boat, accompanied by a flood of Arabic that brought a smile to her lips. It was good to be back beside the Nile again.

A peasant urged his donkey to a faster pace down the track beside the Nile and the reluctant animal broke into a trot, coming to a four-footed stop beside a channel with which it was obviously familiar. The peasant removed a cylindrical object from across the donkey's back and Lucy watched with interest as he sat with his feet in the water, drawing up the water to irrigate his plot of land just behind her.

So intent was she in watching him turn the handle and the trickle of water which wound its way up the screw and into the channel that she didn't notice a second person making his way down the track until he was practically on top of her. She stood up hurriedly to avoid being trodden on, as surprised to see him as he was to see her.

"Mrs. Jameson?"

She nodded briefly, annoyed at the way he was looking at her. She had grown wary of men who gave every woman they met a sexual appraisal whether they wanted to follow through or not. It reminded her of things better forgotten, things that made her shudder inwardly at their memory although she was now in complete charge of her own life and owed nothing to anyone, not even for their company. Then she shrugged, reflecting that two could play at that game, and gave him look for look, a slight frown creasing her brow as she noticed the distaste in his eyes. Her attention was diverted almost immediately by the discovery that those eyes were of almost exactly the same hue as the waters of the river behind her. Something of what she had been thinking must have shown on her face for an answering gleam of amusement flickered in those green-speckled eyes and he ran an impatient hand through his already ruffled, corn-coloured hair.

"I thought you belonged to him for a moment," he said, jerking his thumb towards the peasant.

Lucy squinted at him against the setting sun. She was dark for an English woman, her hair almost black and her eyes of so dark a brown that her husband had asked her once if she had gypsy blood in her veins. She tightened her mouth in irritation, banishing the brief recollection with an effort that made her clench her two hands into fists by her side.

"I don't think he'd be flattered," she answered. "The fellah hasn't veiled herself for years, but her ideas of modesty are a trifle old-fashioned for my taste."

The man's face relaxed into a smile of appreciation as his glance travelled upwards from her sandals, past well-shaped legs, to a slim waist and a full bosom. His eyes lingered on her high cheekbones before settling on her curly dark hair.

"*Mrs.* Jameson," the man repeated. "What does Mr. Jameson do while you indulge yourself in Egypt?"

"There is no Mr. Jameson," she replied shortly.

"Divorced?"

"Widowed. Not that it's any of your business. What does your Mrs. What's-your-name do while you travel about, filming this and that?"

"There is no Mrs. Naseby," he answered as she had.

She lifted disbelieving brows. "Divorced?"

"I'm a bachelor. Jonathan Naseby, as if you didn't know. Remember me? I'm the TV producer who's hired you to front a series on *Life and Death in Ancient Egypt.*"

"Mr. Naseby," Lucy acknowledged. "What

made you choose me?" she asked curiously. "You do do the choosing, don't you? Isn't that what the producer does?"

"Right. I'm the one who sets up the project, chooses the director, in this case, myself, gets it all okayed by our TV bosses, and generally puts the framework together that makes the filming possible. I chose you, Mrs. Jameson, because I was assured that you could make Ancient Egypt come alive to a class of imbeciles and that you were a looker as well."

"I see," she said coolly. So that accounted for his long, appraising look! "You don't seem to have a very high regard for your audience!"

His lips twisted cynically. "I'm a realist, Mrs. Jameson. I know that in a year's time they'll have forgotten almost everything we've tried to put across to them. If they do remember anything, it'll be some detail you were rather hoping they'd forget."

"I expect they'll remember Akhenaton and Nefertiti—especially Nefertiti! She was so very beautiful—"

"And Cleopatra and the asp," he interrupted dryly. "Beautiful women are always memorable, even when they have mud on their faces." He lifted a hand and brushed her cheek with a force that startled her. It was like a charge of electricity going through her.

"Are we doing Cleopatra and the asp?" she asked. She rubbed her cheek thoughtfully where the splash of mud had been. "You know I can only think of one representation of Cleopatra anywhere in Egypt and she's far from beautiful in that. I'd rather leave her out. She's not at all mainstream and will just confuse the issue."

"Indeed?"

"She was a Ptolemaist. On the death of Alexander the Great, his generals divided up his conquests between them and Ptolemy received Egypt as his share. He called himself Pharoah, but his culture was Greek not Egyptian, and that goes for Cleopatra, too. She doesn't come into the real history of Ancient Egypt any more than her representation in the temple is more than a poor copy of an art form whose time had come and gone."

Jonathan Naseby gave way gracefully, or at least, she hoped that was what he was doing.

"We can work out the content of each programme when we're not standing up," he suggested. "I suppose there is someplace nearby where we can sit down?"

"The hotel where you're staying is very comfortable—"

"I understand you're not staying there, however?"

"Well, no," she admitted. "I'm staying with an old friend." Let him think about that, she thought with inward amusement. Egypt was an old stamping ground of hers and, surely, that must give her some advantage. "If you want to get started right away, though, I'm sure Suleiman will oblige us with a couple of chairs and some lemonade. He doesn't keep anything stronger."

She walked ahead of him, a slight swagger in her step, convinced she had found a weak spot when she had mentioned lemonade. That would hurry him away to his hotel! If he wanted a whisky, he wouldn't get it anywhere in the village because Suleiman, though a Copt by religion, had lived among Moslems for so long that the only alcoholic beverage that ever passed his lips was the Communion wine in church.

"You're on," said Jonathan Naseby.

"For lemonade?" she threw over her shoulder.

"For whatever you care to offer me," he responded meekly.

Lucy was glad she was meeting this man for strictly professional reasons. He had an aura of masculinity that might have been hard to cope with under other circumstances. She, of all people, ought to know how easy it was to be mistaken by the outward appearances of a man. If Jonathan Naseby weren't dangerous, he would be married by now and not on the prowl, looking for easy conquests to feed his male ego. If she had known how young he was, she might not have agreed to do the television series at all. She had been tempted by the fee, as she had long had a dream of mounting an expedition of her own in Nigeria. There she had a better chance of making a name for herself than here in Egypt, where sometimes all that seemed left to do was to dot the *i*'s and cross the *t*'s of somebody else's work.

The courtyard of Suleiman's house was small and packed full of women and children who all stood up at their coming, scuttling off into the privacy of the house beyond. The women wore mostly black, with black or white scarves covering their heads. The boys were dressed in pyjamas, the girls in shifts of the same material. Some of them still had their school overalls on, making splashes of bright blue against the predominately dun colour of the whole village.

Lucy seated herself on one of the insecure green painted chairs, keeping an eye on Jonathan to see his reaction to his surroundings. Immediately she wished she hadn't. He took the chair opposite her, very much at his ease, rubbing one hand over his chest beneath his half open shirt. The action drew her attention to the breadth of his shoulders and his powerfully packed muscles. She took a deep breath and looked away. This was *business*, she reminded herself.

"Lemonade, Mr. Naseby?"

He nodded. "Jonathan," he corrected her. He looked about him, his eyes narrowing as he took in the giggling children peering at him from every vantage point in the house. "Are you sure you want to stay here?"

"Why not?" She felt as prickly as a porcupine.

"It might be difficult to concentrate with so much going on. Also, you might not be proof against the water. I had a look at the village pond coming in. People were gathering water from it despite the green slime on it. Is that what you're given to drink here?"

Lucy grinned. "The slime is reputed to be good for the fertility of both women and animals—"

"Really?"

To her annoyance, Lucy blushed. "There's also a water tower that provides the village with clean water," she said quickly. "You don't have to worry about me. You're just as likely to go down with a bug at your classy hotel."

"You haven't told me why you're not staying there."

She threw back her head in a proud gesture that any member of her family would have instantly recognised.

"No, I haven't!"

"Have you got something against hotels?"

"No."

"Well, then?"

She wished the insistence in those river-coloured eyes were less disturbing to her. He was a good-looking devil, as Miles had been, but what was that to her? She had no intention of getting involved with him or any other man ever again. She was happy with the life she had made for herself as a professional woman. She had vowed the day she had been widowed she would never make herself a hostage to somebody else's fortune ever again. She would make her own way in the world, independent and, above all, *free!* After Miles, any man who could make her heart flutter with a look was definitely suspect and somebody to be avoided.

"I prefer to be with friends," she said shortly. She stood up abruptly. "I'll fetch some lemonade."

She knew he was watching her every movement as she disappeared into the house and came back with a jug of cold water, some lemons, sugar, and a couple of glasses on a tray.

"Have you been here all day?" he asked.

Lucy cast a quick, anxious look across the courtyard to where she had thrown the *helaliyeh,* the voluminous garment most Egyptian country-women wrap around themselves when they go out. For some reason she didn't want him to know she had arrived a day early and had been lent the anonymous garment when she had insisted on accompanying the family out into the fields that morning. She didn't think Jonathan would understand the pleasure it gave her to dig the earth, to plant and reap the crops alongside the others. Most people would think her mad to relish the back-breaking work, which was just as much a part of life now as it always had been beside the Nile.

"I went out with the family earlier," she compromised. "They grow fantastic vegetables around here, huge and tasty. I recommend them to you."

"Is that how you got mud on your face?"

She handed him his glass of lemonade. "I assure you I won't have mud on my face by the time your cameras are ready to roll," she said.

As she leaned over the table, his hand, far from accepting the proffered glass, brushed against her cheek, dislodging a flake of mud that fell onto the table between them. Lucy put the glass down with a jerky movement and ran an agitated hand through her short curls. That was another thing about men, she thought with irritation, they made far too much about any female's appearance, as if they didn't think a woman had any other purpose but to primp and worry as to whether her looks were having the desired effect on some man! What did having mud on her face have to do with her qualifications as an archeologist?

"I was wondering if it were a bit of Ancient Egyptian makeup?" he murmured.

Her antagonism died, a touch of mischief stirring in its place. "I'll tell you about Ancient Egyptian makeup if you like," she offered, and proceeded to do so—at length.

She told him all about the wooden toilet case of Tutu, the wife of the scribe Ani, which was now in the British Museum. She explained how popular the "doe-eyed" look had been, mentioned the silver tweezers with which Tutu had tweaked out her excess eyebrows, and told exactly how she would wet the tip of her finger, or the end of a little brush, and dip it into the little bottle containing kohl, and how she would have drawn a ring round each eye, applying a thicker coating to her eyelids.

When she paused for breath, Jonathan Naseby was sitting back in his chair watching her through half-closed lids.

"Are you planning to make up like that for the benefit of the great British public?" he asked.

She was taken aback by the question. "Would they be interested?"

"Fascinated. You go through the motions with such spirit. I can see you're a natural for presenting the past to a reluctant audience. What else did Tutu do to her appearance?"

Lucy took a deep breath to steady herself, self-conscious now that she had his whole interest. Somehow, it was no longer a game: it was the next best thing to an audition. She felt on trial and didn't like the feeling.

She shrugged, the life going out of her performance. "She'd have put red ochre on her lips and cheeks. And use henna to tint her nails, and to redden the palms of her hands and the soles of her feet. It's still done today on special occasions— mostly in the country. Sometimes they draw patterns with the henna, hoping it'll bring them good luck."

"You'll be telling me next that they had mud-packs and beauty parlours!"

She resisted the taunt. He might pretend to be bored by the subject, but she knew his attention was firmly held, if only because he wanted a taste of what she would offer in the programmes.

"They had a mud-pack treatment based on powdered alum. I don't know about beauty parlours. I think they made up most of their own perfumes. They lacked our modern fixatives, of course, but they had any number of scented oils that they used then, and which are still to be found in the small parfumeries of Cairo. Tutu had a charming alabaster bottle in which she kept whichever one she was using. She probably bathed in asses' milk from time to time, as Cleopatra was reputed to have done, but bathing was more probably anointing her skin with the milk rather than filling the tub with it."

"Pity," he said. "I should have enjoyed seeing you splash around in a marble bath filled with milk."

"Neither Tutu, nor anyone else, would do her bathing in public, Mr. Naseby," she said coldly.

A muscle twitched in his cheek. "Jonathan," he prompted her.

"Mr. Naseby," she repeated. "I'd have to know you a lot better before I started calling you Jonathan."

One moment he was seated on the painted wooden chair, the next he was on his feet, leaning across the torn plastic-topped table and grasping her hands in one of his.

"Suits me," he said. "I've an itch to get to know you better, too, Mrs. Jameson. You're a mighty attractive woman, despite the mud on the end of your nose!"

She had a breathless view of the strong line of his jaw and the sensuous curve of his upper lip before he slipped around the table and reached his other hand round her, planting itself firmly on the small of her back, only to travel upwards beneath her T-shirt, discovering the smooth silkiness of her bare skin. His brows rose slightly as he realised she had nothing on beneath the crumpled cotton of her shirt and the hot colour came stinging up her neck and into her face as he began a more intimate exploration.

"Let me go, Mr. Naseby," she commanded in an icy tone.

He did so. He was breathing harder than he had been before, she noticed, although he looked as calm as ever on the surface. Lucky him, she thought, as she struggled to maintain her own cool. If she had felt the sudden heat in his body, he must have been equally aware of the wild, unwelcome response that had coursed through hers at his touch.

"How long have you been widowed, Lucy Jameson?"

"What has that got to do with anything?"

He sat down again. "I can understand your

being annoyed, but not *surprised*. You must know you're the most attractive woman to come my way in a long time?"

Her eyes widened in astonishment. "Don't be ridiculous!"

His smile was wry. "You must have been widowed a mighty long time if you don't know how any unattached man would feel about you."

Lucy gasped. "I'm not even pretty!"

"No," he agreed, completely under control once again, "you're not pretty, nothing so banal, thank God. You have the kind of face a camera loves, where being pretty isn't much of a help. You'll be able to make a whole career in television by the time I've finished with you—if you want to. Do you?"

"I don't know."

She couldn't bring her mind to bear on what he was saying. She was too involved with her own thoughts and the painful worry that he was the first man in a long, long time who'd been able to knock a hole in her defenses against his whole sex. And he hadn't really been trying! She was suddenly vulnerable and she didn't like the feeling. Nor did she like to be as conscious of anyone as she was of Jonathan Naseby. She knew his every feature as if she had been examining him under a magnifying glass.

She looked away. "If the programmes come off as they should, the audience will be listening to what I'm saying, not concentrating on me. They won't really notice me at all."

His sudden laughter shocked her. "My dear girl, television accentuates every attribute, especially those you most want to keep hidden. You can be as retiring as you wish, you'll still be revealed as the sexiest archeologist on two legs! What else did you expect?"

"A job, that's all. I needed the money."

He stood up again, his body tense and on the alert. She retreated a couple of steps, turning her back on him.

"I can promise you money," he said. "What are you going to give me in return?"

"Ancient Egypt with a human face, what else?"

Jonathan swallowed his lemonade in a single gulp. He walked across the courtyard and picked up her borrowed *helaliyeh,* examining it with interest. When he had satisfied his curiosity, he threw it over her shoulders, imprisoning her close beside him. She caught the edges of the cloth and drew the garment closer about her, lifting it up to cover her head as well.

"Walk with me through the village to where I left my car," he said. "We can fix up a time tomorrow when we can discuss the first few programmes in detail. All right? Each installment has to last exactly fifty minutes, including credits, etcetera. Think you can manage some kind of an outline of the first two by then?"

"I sent you some notes—"

He grabbed her arm through the rough material of the black robe. "I read them, Lucy, but I need persuading that you know how to divide up your material. Lecturing a class of students who are already hooked on the subject is quite different from making a dead culture come alive to non-experts who only really want to know if Egyptian mummies are anything like the ones they saw in the horror movie the week before. We'll need a lot more than the dry facts you put in those notes."

She had no time to answer for, at that moment, a turbanned Suleiman came into the courtyard, saluting as smartly as he ever had in the days when he had been attached to the British Army.

Lucy greeted him in Arabic, looking suitably demure when he answered her in his own brand of stilted English.

"I was told you are entertaining a friend, Miss Lucy. You should have told me and I'd've come out to you before. Is he known to your family?"

Lucy introduced Jonathan as the television producer who was employing her. "He's not staying," she added dryly. "He prefers the comfort of a hotel."

Suleiman chose to be impressed by his visitor's importance. "Such a man will have stayed in the very best hotels all over the world! However, if you will honour my house tomorrow, sir, we shall make a feast that will make the whole village happy to see you. We will make a fine meal of duck and couscous, and some of the vegetables Miss Lucy helped us get ready for market this morning. We'll have a very happy evening!"

Lucy held her breath, afraid of what Jonathan might say. She cast him a quick, half-pleading look and was rewarded by the tightening of his hand on her arm.

"I can see why Lucy prefers to stay with you and your family," he said easily, shaking Suleiman's extended hand. "I'd very much like to come tomorrow. Can I bring something for the feast?"

Suleiman expanded visibly. "Life is very modern now in Egypt and we have everything we need here, in the village, close to hand. We have piped water now—everything!"

"Soon you'll be as advanced as your ancestors," Lucy couldn't resist interjecting. "It was the Ancient Egyptians who invented the tap!"

"We're the same people, Miss Lucy," Suleiman reminded her. "In my church, we even speak the same language."

"Arabic?" Jonathan asked.

"No, sir, the language of the ancient Pharaohs."

Jonathan's interest was caught. It was some time later and only after many polite farewells before he went to leave. Lucy accompanied him to the edge of the village.

"How did you ever get to know an old soldier

like Suleiman?" he asked Lucy. "I can't believe
he's ever worked on an archeological site!"

Lucy smiled. "He was my father's batman,"
she explained. "I hope you realize, by the way,
how much trouble he'll go through tomorrow on
your behalf. And he's not a rich man either—"

"I do," Jonathan replied. "I'm very honoured.
But don't forget, we have to see each other first.
I'll expect you the first thing in the morning."

Lucy made a face. "Eight o'clock too early for
you?"

"Fine," he agreed. "I'll treat you to breakfast."
He opened the door to his car. "Good night,
Lucy. Sweet dreams!" He dropped a light kiss on
her cheek, then folded himself into his car and
drove off without a backward glance.

Chapter Two

Lucy dressed with care for her appointment the following morning, selecting a scarlet smock dress, with white collar and cuffs, which set off her dark colouring. She crammed her papers in a leather briefcase that her family had given her when she had qualified, carrying off the honours of her year, thus making herself financially independent of the husband they had lived to regret pressing her to marry. They had all been as impressed with the rich, dashing young man as she had been herself. Miles had been rich, romantic, and a good-enough racing driver to be a household name. It had seemed like a miracle to Lucy when he had chosen her for his wife.

The hotel where Jonathan was staying had known many famous names among its clientele. Lucy had never stayed there herself, but she had visited often enough to be immediately recognised by the staff as she entered.

"Mr. Naseby is expecting you, Mrs. Jameson. You'll find him in the dining room."

There is always a moment of tension when entering a public room on one's own. Was that why her pulse quickened as she made her way to where Jonathan was sitting?

"Am I late?" she asked him.

Smiling politely, he rose. "No, my secretary hasn't surfaced yet. What will you have for breakfast?"

She refused the traditional cooked English breakfast, electing instead some fruit juice and coffee, rounded off with some of the local bread still hot from the oven.

"I didn't realise you had your secretary with you," she said.

"I don't. This is some girl I hired in Cairo to take notes while we talk. If she doesn't come down soon, however, it looks as though we'll have to manage without her."

All business now, Lucy opened her briefcase and took out the notes she had made for the first programme of the series.

"Something general, do you think? A sort of résumé of the times, with landmarks like the Exodus. I want to point out how the period of Akhenaton, despite the attention paid to it, was really just a ripple in the mainstream religion of Egypt. Of course we'll come to it later in some detail, but a survey of the whole period would be appropriate, starting with the first king of the Two Lands—"

Jonathan shuffled through the notes she had prepared for him earlier. "The importance of tradition is what you have here. I thought you were going to peg the argument on Egyptian art. Is that right?"

She nodded. "Especially religious art."

"Okay, I'll go along with that. I suppose it means filming all over Egypt?"

"Well, yes, but it won't be too bad. Once I have the scripts written, mostly one for each place, I thought the first and the last programmes could be filmed as we go along. Can't we do that?"

"If you can get it scripted with the right camera angles, we can."

Lucy chewed on her lower lip. "I don't know enough about filming to do that on my own."

"That's what I figured," he said. "I, if not my secretary, am at your disposal."

"I didn't know directors did that sort of thing," Lucy said.

"Directors find themselves doing a bit of everything more often than not." He eyed her thoughtfully. "I shall enjoy working with you, Lucy Jameson, but I think I may enjoy playing with you more."

Lucy took a sip of coffee. "I don't play," she said. "I gave it up in my salad days. To tell you the truth, I never found it much fun."

"No?"

She wished she could make out what he was thinking, but his expression was bland.

"It's probably hard for a man like you to believe that a woman can find her satisfaction in her work, but I assure you that it's so with me. I'm never happier than when I'm digging up some artifact, or discovering something new about some dead and buried civilisation."

His eyes swept over her. "Why are you afraid of the living?" he asked so gently that she was taken aback.

Defensively she asked, "What makes you think I am?"

"The way your hackles rise every time I try to get near you. You should have been over your husband's death by now. How long is it? Two years? So I keep asking myself why you're so defensive. It could be a bad experience in your recent past, but I don't think so—"

"It could be that I don't like the look of *you*, Mr. Naseby. Have you thought of that?"

He smiled. "I rejected that answer almost immediately. You like the look of me as much as I do you. It's more likely that your husband gave you a bad time. Is that it?"

Lucy veiled her eyes and deliberately stilled her agitated breathing. "Miles was tall, dark, and handsome and very rich as well. I was over the moon with joy when he asked me to marry him."

"And how old were you then?"

"Eighteen. I'd just started at university." She turned defiant eyes on him. "We married almost straight away, but I went on with my studies just the same. I had plenty of time. Miles was away racing a lot of the time and he didn't want me with him then—"

"You were lonely?"

"No, of course I wasn't lonely! I had my own career to worry about!"

"And you were what when he died? Twenty-six?"

She recovered herself with difficulty. "We hadn't seen each other for six months when he was killed. Racing was in his blood. He went in for all the championship events during the season, but even in the off-season he would be flying round the world looking for other less-well-known races. The other Grand Prix drivers were always telling him that his attitude was irresponsible. He didn't want to prove the car, or the team, only himself. He'd take the most appalling risks and then, one day, he took too many. It was lucky he didn't kill anyone else. He didn't care whom he put in jeopardy if he could gain an extra inch in what he called the battle of nerves."

Jonathan was watching her. "I suppose he lived his life the same way?"

"Yes, he did." She sighed, wishing she could recall the admission. "He never took no for an answer."

"That could be said of any thrustful, confident man."

"And of any child trying to gain adult attention."

There was a long silence, then Jonathan asked, "Why did you marry him?"

"I was flattered to be asked—and I wanted children."

That had been a major source of ill feeling between them, she remembered dully. Miles had thought of marriage as an extension of his bachelor days. It was good to have someone close to him, who could always be relied on to be there, but it had made no difference to the way he lived. Lucy had always suspected that it had been a case of out of sight, out of mind as far as she had been concerned. After a while she had lost interest in what he was doing when he was away, she had been miserable enough on the rare occasions when he had been at home.

"You were scarcely more than a child yourself!"

Lucy scarcely heard the comment. She favoured Jonathan with a blank stare, putting her memories behind her with difficulty. She managed a wan smile of apology.

"I don't know why I should've told you that," she said. "I usually pretend it was a time of sunshine and roses all the way. Married to Miles Jameson! What more could any girl want?"

"Someone to love you?" he suggested.

Tears came into her eyes and she brushed them away angrily. "Work is far more reliable and satisfying!" she claimed.

He shook his head at her. "Not true, as I shall hope to demonstrate to you sooner or later—probably sooner if you look at me like that! Ah, here comes my secretary!" His smile was wry with self-mockery. "Saved by the bell, Mrs. Jameson. Don't count on always being so lucky."

The children came running out to greet her when Lucy got back to the village. She was never sure which had been fathered by Suleiman and which were his grandchildren, for Amina, his wife, was considerably younger than he, his first wife having died many years before.

It was Amina, though, who was the most determined to gain her attention. "You have a visitor! Your sister is here. How is it we have never seen her before?"

Lucy was as surprised as her hostess. "Faye? What brings her here?" She swung the child she was holding down to the ground, unclasping his eager fingers from the collar of her dress. "Is she alone?"

Amina shrugged expressive shoulders. "She had trouble finding the right house. She seems upset."

Lucy hurried down the path towards Suleiman's house, the children running after her, the noise they were making reverberating through the overheated air.

"Why didn't you tell me you were coming?" Lucy greeted Faye with a hug.

"I wasn't sure I'd have time to visit." Her sister wrinkled up her nose. "Egypt isn't your exclusive territory! Seb and I came on holiday. Doing the Nile is very much the done thing among our friends these days."

"I shouldn't have thought it to be your scene," Lucy said.

"No. Seb wanted to come. It's our last fling together as a matter of fact. We're splitting up."

The smile left Lucy's face. "Why? I thought you were happy together?"

"You never were a very good judge of these things," Faye said with sisterly candour. "Sebastian has found somebody new, that's all. I'm told she was a great success at the office party last Christmas. Are you beginning to make out without Miles?"

"I'm working hard."

"So what's new? What am I going to do, Lucy? I've never had a career of my own and I'm not sure I could handle one now."

"I thought you loved Seb," Lucy said, bewildered.

"Love is a two-way street. I'd've thought your experience with Miles would have taught you that."

Lucy drew her sister into the relative privacy of

the courtyard of Suleiman's house. "I learned that being a man's wife gave one a certain advantage. Passing fancies are apt to do just that, you know, pass!"

"Seb isn't Miles!"

"What's that supposed to mean?"

"Nothing." Faye managed to look both sulky and uncomfortable. "Seb and I always said we'd let the other one go if it came to it. Only, I never expected to be held to the bargain. I *like* being Mrs. Sebastian Morris! I don't want to have to share the name with somebody else. It's mine! Seb gave it to me, so how can he take it back again now?"

Lucy sank into the nearest chair. "Doesn't Sebastian matter more than his name?"

Faye smiled a sour smile. "They both matter. Look at you! I was reading an article about this series you're making: Lucy Harris, it said, in real life Mrs. Miles Jameson. It's a man's world, my love. You're not real when you're using your own name!"

"I use both names—"

"Not professionally, you don't! How Miles hated that! He always went into one of those black rages of his when he heard you referred to as Professor Lucy Harris."

"Funny," said Lucy, "I never noticed. Most of the people I work with seem to call me Mrs. Jameson these days. Jonathan does—did—when he calls me anything."

Her sister cocked an eyebrow. "Jonathan?"

"Jonathan Naseby, the producer I'm working with."

"Ah!" There was a wealth of meaning in that one syllable. "Do I get to meet the great man?"

"If you stay to dinner."

"Before then, by the sound of things," Faye said, amused by Lucy's agitated expression. "Isn't he here now?"

Lucy knew by the prickle of electricity on the back of her neck that it was he indeed. She felt herself colour and hoped her usually observant sister would be too involved with her own affairs to notice.

"What a pity you should arrive just now," Faye greeted him, flicking her auburn hair into shape with one hand. "Lucy was about to tell me all about you—from her point of view, of course."

Jonathan advanced across the courtyard, completely at his ease. "She doesn't know much about me—yet," he said.

Faye patted the chair beside her. "I'm Faye Morris, Lucy's elder sister. We like to keep an eye on her since she was widowed, in case she gets up to something she shouldn't. My husband may be along later."

Jonathan shook hands with her and sat down. "Is that really why you're here?"

Faye's eyes fell before his. "Not entirely. Does it matter?"

Jonathan sat back, shrugging out of his jacket.

"Not really. Anyhow, to set your fears at rest, Lucy's in my care and quite safe."

Lucy stared at him. "I'm not in anyone's care, thank you very much. If anyone's in need of care, it's both of you! At least I'm at home here—"

"Speaks the language like a native," her sister added.

Jonathan laughed. "Suleiman would be chaperon enough for anyone. Was he really your father's batman?"

It was Faye who answered him. "Father was involved in guarding the Suez Canal at one time. Mother hated it out here and I don't remember it at all. Lucy is the only one to make it her stamping ground for months every year."

Lucy said nothing. She could feel Jonathan's eyes on her face, boring into her head as if he would read her private thoughts with as much ease as if they were his own. She knew then that it was going to be a thoroughly tiresome evening. Biting back the comment that one could hardly be an Egyptologist if one never spent any time in Egypt, Lucy pretended to herself that she was glad Jonathan and her sister were getting on so well. Miles and Faye had got along well, too. Miles had admired Faye's warm colouring and flirtatious ways. He had often held her sister up as an example of all that a wife should be. *She* didn't hang round Sebastian all day and night. She found her own interests and understood when Sebastian wanted to be off on his own.

"I think I'll go and help Amina," she said aloud, but as she made to get up, Jonathan's hand closed round her wrist and drew her back down onto her seat.

"What made you choose Egypt?" he asked her.

"I don't know."

Faye's glance was malicious as it rested on Jonathan's hand. "Let her go, Jonathan. She was always peculiar about Egypt, even as a child. Miles used to say the only time he saw her really get excited was at the prospect of unearthing a dead mummy. No man could possibly compete with a pyramid where she's concerned."

"Perhaps they never tried," Jonathan answered dryly, releasing her hand abruptly.

Lucy was glad to make her escape. Her wrist burned where Jonathan had held it and she rubbed it with her other hand, a bitter look on her face. If she had escaped from her marriage into her other love in life, so had Miles. She had thought at first it was speed he had worshipped, but she had soon learned better. That had been a necessary part of the whole package. It had been the adulation he had been truly hooked on; there had been nothing he had enjoyed more than having his shirt torn off by a howling pack of teenagers, all hoping to catch his attention for a fleeting moment. That had been about as long as her husband could sustain a serious relationship, she thought grimly.

Suleiman looked up as she darted through the

main room of the house, which was also the kitchen, on her way to her own room.

"Are you getting hungry, Miss Lucy?"

"I'm getting worried about numbers," she called back to him. "Faye's husband may be along later—"

"There's plenty of everything," he reassured her. "How many more plates will we need? I'll send Youssuf out to borrow three more, shall I?"

Lucy appeared in the door of her room. "I'm sorry about this. I didn't know they were in Egypt, let alone that they would turn up here."

Suleiman shrugged. "They're all welcome, though I'd have liked you to have had time alone with this new man of yours. Don't let other people's troubles spoil it for you."

"He's hardly mine, Suleiman," Lucy said. "I'm working with him, nothing more."

"There's time yet."

Lucy was sadly shaken by this exchange. She had been busily telling herself that it was entirely in her imagination that Jonathan was being other than polite by paying her compliments. She felt suddenly vulnerable and unsure of herself. She was a bad chooser when it came to men and she couldn't bear to be hurt again as she had been before. She went back into her room and fished about in the small lacquered box where she kept her few pieces of jewellry. Her wedding ring gave her no pleasure as she slipped it into place over her knuckle. She could remember the day

she had taken it off and the flood of tears that had
been caused not by grief but with relief that the
years of her bondage to Miles had come to an
end. The band of gold looked strange against her
tanned fingers and she could feel it rubbing where
once it had been quite comfortable. It wouldn't
afford her much protection either, seeing that
everyone knew that Miles was dead, but it might
help her to remember what a few kisses could
lead to, and she needed all the help she could get
to withstand the appeal of Jonathan Naseby.

Lucy came back out into the hive of activity in
the kitchen, smiling with envy at the busy family
who, whether they lived there or not, seemed to
belong in a way that had been forgotten in the
West. Everyone had his own task and performed
it with a will. Usually, it was the small girls of the
family who were sent out daily to collect animal
dung from the roads, which they made into flat
cakes to be used to fire the stove in one corner of
the room. There was never enough fuel to be had
though, and the great piles of maize stalks and
cotton sticks that were stored up on the roof were
used to eke it out. Someone had recently brought
a bundle down the steps and had left a trail of dust
across the floor. In another moment, when
Amina saw it, there would be a shriek of dismay
and it would be gone in a moment under the fury
of her broom.

Reluctant to go back to the others, Lucy asked
if there was anything she could do, knowing her

offer would be dismissed with contempt because Amina had long ago discovered her inability to keep the stove properly stoked, let alone balance the half-dozen pots and pans on the top in the right order so that everything would be cooked at the same time.

"Go and talk to your visitors," she was bidden. "Your sister's husband has arrived. Go, before your man gets impatient with your absence! They were never meant to be friends, those two!"

Faye was holding forth on their childhood when Lucy moved out of the shadows into the sunlit light of the courtyard.

"Lucy used to *live* in the British Museum as a child," she recalled. "I always thought it positively gruesome to be fascinated by mummies and ruined temples and things like that! She never had any boyfriends that I can remember. She wouldn't have noticed Miles if he hadn't almost run her over in the street."

Lucy joined in the general laughter, wishing she could find any real amusement at the memory.

"He thought the public highways were his personal racing tracks," she said out loud, trying to keep the bitterness out of her voice. "Fortunately, he was banned from driving for most of the time I was married to him."

"Did you ever watch him race?" Jonathan asked her.

"Once."

"Once was enough," Faye agreed unexpectedly. "He was a monster when he got behind the wheel of a car."

"Not only then," Sebastian said abruptly. "How are you doing, Lucy?"

Lucy murmured something noncommital.

Jonathan had heard this brief exchange. Soon after, he took her to one side, his eyes going immediately to her restored wedding ring.

"Is it possible to see the sun set from the roof?" he asked her.

She nodded, gesturing towards the sunbaked staircase that went up the outside of the house.

"Then let's go," he said.

"I can't leave the others—"

"Nonsense! They don't seem to be thinking that much about you." He caught her by the left hand, pulling her angrily after him and crushing her fingers against her ring. "That isn't what's worrying you, Lucy. They can have their fight without you and you know it. You just don't want to be alone with me."

"What makes you think that?" Lucy asked crossly.

He put an arm round her shoulders and pulled her hard up against him. The shock of the contact knocked her breath out of her. A wave of desire for him passed through her. She tried to fight it by closing her eyes, but then she had no distractions from his warm, masculine smell and the feel of his body against hers.

"Did Miles wear a ring, too?"

She opened her eyes, shocked. "No. No, of course not. He didn't like his fans to know he was married."

She tried to concentrate on the scene about them. The evenings in Egypt were her favourite time of day, when the whole world was bathed in light and the sky was streaked in red and gold in equal proportions. Looking east, there was the land of the living, the neat fields, the palms, and the animals, everything that went to sustain the hard lives of the people of the Nile. Looking west, on the other hand, one could see the arbitrary line that separated the black soil of the annual inundation from the sands of the desert. It was on the western side that the dead had been buried.

Lucy could hear Faye berating Sebastian for something. She was glad Jonathan had suggested that they leave them alone.

"Look," she whispered, "isn't the sun enormous as it slips down below the horizon? Isn't it beautiful?"

"So are you," said Jonathan, and he lowered his head to touch his lips to hers.

"Don't!" Lucy rebuked him sharply.

His arms brought her hard up against the wall of his chest and then he was kissing her again and she forgot all about the foolishness of getting involved with him. She put her arms up around his neck and kissed him back with enthusiasm. It wasn't at all like being kissed by Miles. Jonathan's kiss was like sheet lightning, a blaze of glory in a darkened world.

"If I were you, I'd put that ring away again," he said, smiling into her eyes as he set her free. "It won't do you any good where I'm concerned."

"I didn't put it on for your benefit!" She pushed away from him as hard as she could.

"Didn't you?" he said. "I thought you did." He took her hand and held it between them. "Take it off, Lucy, and tell me the legend of the sun instead. With your sister downstairs, I'm hardly likely to make love to you here, and when I do, wearing your wedding ring is the last thing that'll stop me!"

Chapter Three

"Is the fact that everyone was buried in the Western Desert the origin of the saying 'going west'?"

"I think they were buried on the western side because the sun dies daily in the west and comes back to the living again in the east. He spent his night travelling through the Kingdom of Osiris among the dead. If you were found worthy, you were allowed to sail with him in his splendid boat."

"Ah, yes," said Jonathan. "Osiris was the one who was murdered by his brother and sewn together again by his wife-sister, Isis, the great goddess. I remember from this morning."

"Their son, Horus, was rather important, too," Lucy told him. "The Pharoahs claimed to be his reincarnation, among other things, and he was closely associated with the cult of the dead. The canopic jars, where they put the main organs of a body they were mummifying, often have lids that represent his four sons. When you died, your heart was weighed in the scales against the symbol of the goddess Ma'at, which was a feather. Ma'at is sometimes translated as 'truth' in English, but 'sincerity' might be a better translation."

"The Last Judgment?"

"Why not? We get a lot of our imagery from Ancient Egypt, through the psalms and so on." She smiled with a touch of self-mockery. "Perhaps that's why I feel so much at home among them."

"Did Miles share your interest?"

Lucy shook her head. "He would have been happier in Ancient Rome as a charioteer."

Jonathan picked up her left hand, placing it firmly on the parapet before them. The last rays of the sun picked up the gold of her ring, making it flash up into her eyes.

"He dazzled you?" Jonathan asked.

"I suppose he did." She wrenched her hand free and put it behind her back. "Or his money did. He was astonishingly rich, you know."

"You didn't see much of it!"

Lucy blinked, wondering how he could know that. Most people of her acquaintance had concluded she had been left very well off when Miles had been killed.

"Fancy cars come at fancy prices," she said aloud.

"And wedding rings don't?"

"I don't know what you're talking about," she said stoutly.

"Don't you?" The savage note in his voice brought a lump the size of a golf ball into her throat. That was all she needed now, to feel *guilty* about something she couldn't help and which had never bothered her in the least before. "What made you marry him? Couldn't you get him out of your system any other way?"

"I wanted children," she explained simply.

"Did he?"

"He wouldn't even talk about it. Would you mind if we talked about something else?"

He stiffened. "Is that why you're wearing that curtain ring—"

"It's a bit better than that!" she protested.

"Is that why you're wearing it? Because you're still mourning his death?"

"No."

"Then take it off and throw it away. Throw it to the west and be done with it forever. You have your own life to live!"

Lucy hesitated. "I am living my own life. You wouldn't have hired me if I'd been Miles's widow and nothing else. You hired Lucy Harris, not Lucy Jameson. Lucy Jameson isn't any of your business!"

"Isn't she?"

A tremour of apprehension caught her unawares. It was not an unpleasant sensation, but it should have been a warning to her that she was getting in over her head.

She swallowed hard. "You forget, I've had the big romance of my life. It came unstuck in my hand and I don't propose to repeat the experience."

He went off on another track. "Why, if you wanted children, didn't you have any?"

She winced, refusing to answer. "That isn't any of your business either."

His hands on her shoulders were surprisingly gentle, coaxing her into the circle of his arms.

"Lucy, darling, I'm making everything about you my business. Let the dead bury the dead and come alive for me!"

"I can't!"

"Can't, or won't?"

What a question! One of his hands came up to the nape of her neck, cradling her head for his kiss. She shut her eyes tightly, determined not to make it easy for him, but at the first touch of his lips, her resolution shattered, to be replaced by such an urgent desire that she arched against him.

"I think the answer is won't. Can't seems to have taken care of itself!"

"I don't want to get involved with anyone again," she told him.

"Can't you trust me not to hurt you?"

He had already. Her mouth felt strange and not quite her own and her heart was pounding so that she was scarcely able to stand without his support.

"Surely you can find someone else to dally with for the few weeks you'll be in Egypt?"

"Did you never learn to play, Lucy? Must life always be such a serious business?"

She couldn't answer that question. How often had she heard the same complaint from Miles, especially in her quest for motherhood! Now Jonathan felt the same way. It was to be expected. It was always the same with men.

"We'd better go back to the others. They'll wonder what we're doing up here," she said in a tight voice.

Jonathan patted her cheek, shaking his head at her subdued expression. "Does it matter what they think?" he asked her.

"It does to me," she said.

The children clustered about her when she and Jonathan came down from the roof. They were excited about having so many visitors all at once and had a hundred and one questions to put to her as to what they were all doing there. She bent down to their level, glad to have a moment or two longer to pull herself together before she had to face Faye and Sebastian once more. Suleiman came to rescue her, pulling them away from her like so many burrs.

"You shouldn't encourage them! Enough, Mahmoud! Go to your mother!"

Lucy laughed at him. "They tell me far more interesting things about Egypt than you do!" she teased him.

"You spoil them!" he retorted, clucking over their sticky fingers that were still clinging to her clothes.

"Do leave those children alone!" Faye begged her sister. "We're all waiting to eat. Seb and I can't stay long."

Lucy obediently disentangled herself. As she did so her joy in the moment died under the watchful eyes of Jonathan Naseby. She had forgotten all about him as she had eased herself away from the wriggling group of giggling children. With them she felt completely at home.

"Oh?" she said, running a hand through her ruffled hair. "What time do you two have to be back?"

"The boat sails at ten-thirty." The answer came from Sebastian. He laughed shortly. "It wasn't my idea to come! Faye thought it'd be a good idea. Can't think why! There's a temple round every corner and they're all exactly the same. What d'you see in this place, Lucy? We can't agree on much at the moment, but we are agreed that Ancient Egypt is a monumental bore!"

Lucy smiled at his choice of adjective in case he had intended it to be funny, though she doubted it. In all the years she had known him, Sebastian had never been known to crack a joke.

"I love it. It must be being badly put across to you."

"I don't listen to any of the guides," he confirmed.

"Pity," said Lucy. "You'd like some of the animal pictures I'm sure—and the domestic scenes are charming! In what other ancient civilisation did men and women allow themselves to be represented seated side by side with their arms round each other?"

She raised an eyebrow at Sebastian and he frowned. Sebastian was a businessman, pure and simple, and anything that didn't make money was a bore to him.

"Faye wanted to come," he said. "Has she told you that we're splitting up?"

"I'm sorry," Lucy said. "It's a painful process I know."

Sebastian heaved a sigh. "What can you know about it? It's different when someone dies. *You* don't carry round a load of guilt that everything's probably your own fault."

Lucy managed a tired smile. "Are things going to be so much better apart?" she asked.

"I don't know," Sebastian admitted. "I think we ought to be getting more out of life than we are—either of us! The magic's gone, and I don't see it coming back for either of us."

"Perhaps you expect too much?"

"You think so?"

She nodded soberly. "Yes, I do. You can't expect to be on the crest of a wave all the time. Nobody is."

It was as well that at that moment Suleiman entered and took his seat at the head of the table,

looking for all the world like a patriarch of old in
his long, striped robe and simple white turban,
loosely tied about his head.

"You should have sent us over to the hotel to
eat," she whispered to him, astonished as always
by the incredible hospitality of the poorest of
mankind.

"You are welcome in my house always," he
reassured her.

"Even so, four of us is a bit much. You must tell
me if my being here is a nuisance—"

"You could never be a nuisance, Miss Lucy.
You're one of us! Remember that first day I took
you to see the pyramids?"

They laughed together. Lucy, aged six, had
confidently expected to be transported back in
time to the years when the Pharoahs had held
court. Her disappointment that she was not to
meet living Ancient Egyptians had been pro-
found. Yet, somehow, Suleiman had surmounted
that handicap and had prompted her interest in a
civilisation, laying the foundations of an interest
that had later turned into a career. He hadn't
been able to introduce her to the Pharoahs in
person, but he had made them come alive for her
in every way that mattered. Later on, she had
been able to reverse the process by translating for
him some of the stories and love poems that were
a part of his heritage, written by his ancestors so
many centuries before.

Lucy recalled herself to the present, taking her

own seat beside Suleiman. From it, she could observe her sister without being watched in her turn by anyone other than Jonathan and he was too busy responding to the laughing taunts that Faye was exchanging with both men. It was the kind of conversation that always made Lucy feel shut out. She had never been any good at countering sophisticated remarks that meant nothing and often held a barb that could hurt and linger long after the amused asides had passed on to something else.

Suleiman's wife brought in a basket of the coarse, flat bread that was a part of every Egyptian meal. In the poorer houses it was used as a knife and fork as well as a food. It could easily be folded and dipped into the soft cheese, or one of the many mixtures of seeds and sesame oil that are a favourite all over the Middle East.

Lucy helped herself, splitting the bread and filling it with the hard-boiled eggs that had been put on the table, finding that she was extremely hungry as she bit into the tasty sandwich. She was pleased to see Jonathan following her example with a minimum of fuss. She would have hated it if he had made a mess of eating with his fingers. She had already observed Seb's expression as he regarded the basket of bread.

The bread and eggs were followed by a perfectly roasted duck, served with the universal brown beans, called *fool,* which were cooked overnight in an earthenware dish and mixed with oil.

When they had finished eating, Suleiman himself made a brew of mint tea, keeping a special
small teapot on one side because Lucy had never
liked the sugar he poured lavishly in on top of the
crushed mint and boiling water.

Jonathan rose to relieve his hostess of a tray full
of gold-striped glasses, pushing her gently down
on the chair he had just vacated. Faye looked up
at him, her expression an open invitation, but he
came and stood behind Lucy's chair, playing idly
with a strand of curl that had broken loose from
the discipline she had attempted to impose on her
short hair.

"May I join you in your unsweetened tea?" he
asked her.

She turned and looked up at him in surprise,
pulling the curl free of his fingers. "It isn't at all
the thing to drink it as I do. Suleiman will be very
disappointed in you. It's meant to have as much
sugar as mint in it."

"What she means is that no one is allowed to
join her in her favoured position," Faye said.
"Lucy doesn't like to share her life out here. She
wouldn't even share it with Miles!"

Lucy flushed. "It's taken me a long time to train
my Egyptian friends that I don't like sweet drinks.
You're lucky to be having mint tea. The alterna-
tive might have been made from prickly pears and
is absolutely disgusting!"

Seb edged his chair a little closer to Lucy's.

"Tell me more," he invited her. He looked round the table. "It's hard to believe that Lucy was just a little girl when I first knew her. Miles didn't know how lucky he was. *I* wouldn't have made that mistake with you, little Lucy. Perhaps I should've waited for you to grow up?"

Faye's mouth tightened into a disapproving line. "Leave Lucy alone!" she snapped. "The only man she ever wanted was Miles and that was her bad luck!"

"I seem to remember a certain interest on your part, too," her husband reminded her.

"Miles was my brother-in-law. Besides he wasn't grown up enough for me," Faye retorted.

He hadn't been grown up enough for Lucy either, but she hadn't known that in the beginning. She had fallen in love with the packaging: the man underneath, when she had found him, had left her cold. She blinked, very much aware of the warmth of Jonathan's fingers as he explored her collarbone and the area just behind her ears. If he went on like that she would lose her grip on the conversation and she couldn't afford to do that. Her marriage to Miles had been her business and nobody else's. She had never confided her troubles in Faye and she didn't want her to guess what had gone on now. She had her own marital difficulties to get on with. Lucy's were over, dead and buried along with her husband.

"He had his good points," she said aloud. "He

never tried to stop me from making my own career, although it meant us being apart more than we would have been otherwise."

"He wasn't short on other consolations in his life," Faye said. "Still, what man hasn't? I don't suppose you want to talk about him right now?"

"No," Lucy said shortly.

Seb shook his head at her. "It's a mistake for any woman to put her career before her marriage. It's unfeminine."

Lucy's gaze was mocking. "You think so?"

"Somebody has to come second if a marriage is going to work."

"And it should always be the woman?" Lucy asked.

"I think so," he maintained stoutly.

"There's such a thing as compromise," Jonathan put in quietly. "Besides, every situation is different. It's impossible to generalize."

He bent his head as he spoke and Lucy braced herself, half expecting, and more than half hoping, that he was about to drop a kiss on the top of her head. She couldn't prevent the wash of excitement that ran in her bloodstream every time he came near. Why him? And why now? It had been so long since her senses had been stirred by any man that she had almost begun to think of herself as being immune. How much more convenient it would be if she were!

Nor was it the kind of discovery she wished to make with her sister there, not with Faye so unhappy, her own marriage on the rocks. Poor Faye! Lucy only wished there was something she could do to help her, but she and Seb would have to sort out their own problems. It was hard to see her sister uncertain and unhappy. She had always had confidence enough for the two of them. She had always thought that Lucy had given Miles a rough deal and she had never hesitated to say so. Was that why Lucy felt she had to be so cautious in what she said to Faye now? She knew how the best intentioned words could hurt, and how little the outsider could know about anyone else's marriage.

"We ought to be going," Seb said. "We've yet more temples and things to see tomorrow."

"You should've stayed on board and listened to the lecture about them tonight," Lucy told him.

"That'll be the day!" He tapped his watch as though he didn't quite believe the time. "We'll look you up again before we go back to England, Lucy, if I haven't cut and run by then. We'd have done better to have cut the knot cleanly instead of this long drawn-out ordeal, but then, you know Faye!"

Lucy stood up also, regretting the necessity because it broke the contact with Jonathan's fingers. She walked her sister and brother-in-law to the exit and out onto the narrow street.

She waved an airy hand to them as they walked away to where they were expecting their taxi to be waiting for them. She waited until she couldn't

even see their shadows in the darkness, hating
herself because she was afraid to get involved in
her sister's unhappiness. Faye hadn't done much
for her when she had been widowed, it was true,
but that could have been because she had been
genuinely mourning Miles in a way that Lucy
never had. She had done her mourning for the
man she had thought she had married a long, long
time before he had died. She had never wanted to
feel anything ever again!

Lucy turned to go back inside and walked
straight into Jonathan. His arms held her close
against the hardness of his chest.

"I hope you're not expecting me to go, too?"
he said.

She took a deep breath. "You can have coffee
first if you like," she offered.

"And a good-night kiss?"

Lucy wrenched herself free of his embrace.
"Ours is a working relationship," she reminded
him. "Let's keep it that way."

He pulled her into the circle of light that the
kerosene lamp cast in one corner of the courtyard. "You can't run away from your emotions
forever, Lucy."

"I'm not an emotional person," she said firmly.

His eyebrows rose. "I don't think you know
very much about yourself," he said finally.

"And you do, I suppose?"

"Not yet, but I will."

Was that a threat or a promise? A flicker of excitement kindled inside her but she frowned back at him.

"You'll only be disappointed if you get involved with me," she told him, "and then you'll take it out on me. I've been through that once, and once is enough."

His gaze was intent, looking right inside her. She wished she knew what he was seeing, what he was thinking.

"I'm not Miles," he said. "Let's have that coffee, shall we?"

Lucy made it herself, putting up with the good-natured ribbing of Suleiman and Amina with a good grace. "Will you join us?" she asked them, hoping they wouldn't leave her alone with Jonathan again that night. She was far too vulnerable where he was concerned.

They refused, however, with gentle good manners and teasing looks. "He wouldn't thank us for dividing your attention! It's a fine man you have this time!"

"It's *business*, Suleiman," she said sharply, softening the words with a smile.

She spent the time it took to drink her coffee rehearsing in her mind how she would refuse Jonathan's offer either to stay himself or to take her back to his hotel for the night. It didn't help that he looked incredibly handsome in the flickering light from the flame of the lamp. If he insisted she'd be hard put to go on refusing him, she thought. It had been a long time since she had felt anything approaching desire for anyone and she didn't want to get involved. The last time had been too disastrous.

"Come for a walk along the Nile with me?" he suggested.

She swallowed the last of her coffee, meaning to refuse, but when he held out his hand to her, she allowed him to pull her up onto her feet. She could feel his breath on her lips and her whole body screamed out for his kiss.

"What went wrong between you and Miles?" he asked.

Lucy's innards twisted into a tight ball. "What makes you think anything went wrong between us?"

He did kiss her then, a mere touch of his lips to hers, a child's kiss that she fiercely resented.

"Did he love you at all, Lucy? Why did he marry you? Or, more to the point, why did you marry him?"

She leaned against him, the words wrung out of her. "I wanted children, but I can't have them. I'm only half a woman, as he delighted in telling me. I was glad of it in the end. He wouldn't have made much of a father. He wasn't much of a husband, if you really want to know."

He held her close against him and she found herself resting her head against his shoulder as if she had every right to do so.

"I want you, Lucy," he whispered. "Won't you ask me to stay the night?"

"I can't!"

"That's what you think now, but I can wait. Tomorrow is another day." He kissed her lips. "Good night, Professor. Sweet dreams!"

Chapter Four

Lucy could see no point in trying to use the creaking telephone system in anything other than a dire emergency. In her experience it seldom worked and if, by some miracle, the line connected, it was hard to hear a word that was being said. Accordingly, she set off to Jonathan's hotel to leave a message in person that she was spending the day with her sister.

To her surprise he was already up and dressed when she made her way into the reception area, her note in her hand.

"I thought we were having an easy day today," he said, greeting her. "We can't do much more until the crew arrives."

"Seb has gone," she said baldly.

"And?"

"Faye's upset, naturally. I promised I'd spend the day with her. I'll make it up later."

There was a glint of amusement deep in Jonathan's eyes as he regarded her flushed, exaspe-

rated face. "What are you going to do with her?"
he asked.

Lucy sank into a chair. "I wish I knew. I
thought I might take her to Giza. She might like
to do a pyramid, or ride a camel—What are you
laughing at?"

"I was picturing your sister perched on top of a
camel. What else have you thought up for her
entertainment?"

It was all right for him! He didn't have the
ordering of the day which she knew in her bones
was going to be disastrous. Faye would go on and
on about Sebastian's defection, and when she had
finished with him, she was bound to start on
Lucy's own marriage to Miles.

"If you can do so much better, why don't you
come, too?" Lucy suggested. "Faye will be glad to
see you, I've no doubt."

"Nor have I," Jonathan agreed promptly.
"Let's have a cup of strong black coffee to pull us
together before we set forth. I shall enjoy seeing
the pyramids with you, though I suspect Faye will
find them rather boring. Have you thought she
might be better off dealing with her own miseries?
She might feel more at home among the friends
she will have made on the tour."

Lucy blinked. "What you mean to say is that
she finds *me* boring?"

"Shall we say you don't have many interests in
common?"

"But I'm her *sister!*"

"That doesn't make you responsible for her happiness. She might prefer to wander through Cairo. She could get a perfume made up just for her. She'd probably enjoy that more!"

"She might, but I wouldn't. And no one's begging you to join us," she added huffily.

His eyes crinkled at the corners. "Think you can manage without me?"

"I have for a good many years," she reminded him. "Besides, I don't think Faye should leave Egypt without seeing at least one pyramid—"

"And you are just the person to show her one? That's all right with me, just as long as it's clearly understood that I'm coming along to hold *your* hand, not hers."

If that were the case, she might do a lot better to go by herself, Lucy thought. Faye had never enjoyed coming second to her sister, not even with Miles. She liked to be the heroine of every event, with everyone else cast as bit players. What would she make of Jonathan flirting with Lucy?

She cast him an anxious look. "Faye is unhappy—"

He stood, taking both her hands in his and drawing her up to her feet. She could feel the caress of his thumb on the palm of her hand and it gave her so much pleasure that she felt guilty. It was hard to remember that she had no business feeling this way about any man. Miles was dead, but her chosen way of life was alive and she was not about to give it up for any man.

"Don't break yourself up over it," Jonathan said gently, going on to confirm her own thoughts. "You have your own life to lead."

And it didn't include him! She couldn't afford the luxury of emotional relationships, but how was she going to explain that to Jonathan?

Faye wrinkled up her nose in genteel distaste as she regarded the three huge monuments that dominated the group of pyramids on the site.

"I'm glad I didn't live in those days," she commented. "I don't approve of slavery."

"Slavery had nothing to do with it!" Lucy exclaimed indignantly. "It was a collective effort, welcomed by the people themselves. It was very important to them from a religious point of view. The Pharoah was the personification of Horus, don't forget, and if the rites were carried out correctly ensuring his proper entrance into the next world, all those who had served him here would be needed by him there. If he passed into heaven as a full-fledged god, their own eternity was guaranteed. The Egyptians were only interested in death because they were such a life-loving people. They couldn't bear the thought of it all coming to an end."

Faye remained unimpressed. "I suppose you also have some explanation of why all their gods wore those silly animal heads?" she said.

"I have, as a matter of fact," Lucy said. "Mankind—Western man in particular—hadn't yet decided that he was something special, cut off and superior to the rest of creation. The idea of an eternity without any animals, or that they had been put in the world for man's convenience and not in their own right, would have struck ancient man as a blasphemy. Maybe, one day, we'll catch up with them about that."

"You know," said Faye, "you really do have some very peculiar ideas. Next you'll be telling me that heaven is strewn with flowers."

"I think mine may be." Lucy laughed. "Perhaps we each make up our own, our own hell, too."

"No, one needs help with that," Faye retorted. "At the moment I am having able assistance from Sebastian. Oh, look, I can see the pyramids! Can we look at the Sphinx, too?"

"Of course."

The car was left in the care of a group of boys who vowed to defend it from all others of their kind for a small sum for which they bargained as diligently as if it were an international deal. They offered a few scarabs for sale, producing the small blue beetles out of their pockets, together with a few other grimy artifacts, which they hoped to pass off as the real thing.

Jonathan handled the scarabs with interest, turning the small hand-made articles over and over on the palm of his hand.

"What do they mean?" he asked at last.

"They're representations of the dung beetle,

actually," Lucy told him. "When they lay their eggs, they roll them up in balls of mud and push them around in front of them. It was thought that they also pushed the sun up over the horizon in the same way. That made them sacred."

Jonathan bought a couple, allowing Lucy to choose them for him because, just sometimes, a genuine old one could be found among the rest. Faye ignored the transaction, shrugging away from the outstretched hands of the boys as they tried to attract her attention. When one came closer than the others, poking her with a bony finger, she yelped out loud and clung to Jonathan's arm for protection. Lucy was tempted to push her sister away from him by the simple expedient of inserting herself between them. She felt unreasonably angry.

Really, she told herself, this was getting out of hand. Why else had she allowed Jonathan to come if not to cheer up Faye's drooping spirits? Why should she care if he chose to do it by holding her hand?

For the first time in her life, Lucy did not enjoy the experience of plunging into the ill-lit passageway of Cheops's pyramid. Normally her heart lifted within her as she left the hot sunshine outside and took in once again the superb construction of the only one remaining of the Seven Wonders of the Ancient World. She would measure with her eye the huge blocks cut from the quarry of Mokkatam, marvelling at the technolo-

gy involved in building this house of death. Like
visiting any other work of art, it was an ennobling
experience to follow the path of the great Pharoah's sarcophagus up into the exact centre of the
pyramid.

But if Lucy was waiting for some sign of
appreciation from her sister, she was destined to
wait in vain. Faye's high heels made walking
difficult and her only reaction to the gigantic
dimensions of the structure was fright, making
her cling closer to Jonathan than ever.

Cross with herself, and crosser still with Faye,
Lucy made no attempt to explain to them the
main features of this, the largest of all the pyramids in Egypt. It was only when Jonathan exclaimed at the freshness of the air within the
King's Burial Chamber that she roused herself to
tell him of the air shaft that had been built into
the tomb.

"Were mummies supposed to breathe?" he
inquired.

"Of course not! It was to allow the Pharoah's
ka, his soul, if you like, to come and go at will. It
didn't do him much good in this case. The tomb
robbers were here almost before the builders had
left."

Jonathan would have liked to have explored
further. "Are you going to bring all this into your
talk on pyramids?" he asked her.

"Yes, it's in the notes I sent you."

He pressed his hand against the rock of the

chamber. "It didn't mean that much to me when I read it. What architects they must have had!"

Lucy allowed herself a smile of satisfaction. "Didn't they just," she agreed.

Faye began to wail that she felt as though she were being closed in forever and couldn't they go, please, before she fainted away. Lucy did her best to hide her impatience, marvelling that Jonathan seemed to find this a pleasing feminine attitude that required immediate action from him.

"You'll feel better when we get outside again," he assured her. "Shall I help you down the Grand Gallery?"

"Please," said Faye in a small voice. "I feel crushed!"

Lucy turned her back on both of them, leaving them to their own devices. She didn't want to watch her sister clutching Jonathan's arm, nor did she want to observe his willingness to go along with what Lucy considered to be one of the oldest female maneuvers since the beginning of time.

She forced her attention onto the magnificent proportions of the King's Gallery, mentally reviewing her notes as she tried to remember whether she had given any idea of the sheer size of the pyramid to the viewers. It would comfortably hold St. Paul's Cathedral and the whole of the Palace of Westminster in its area, she thought.

Down below her she could hear Faye giggling at something Jonathan had said to her. Neither of them even looked back to see if she was following. They would probably have been happier to have come without her, she thought with a pang of bitterness.

"Lucy!"

She jerked back to reality, hurrying to catch up with them. Faye was standing on her own feet by the time she came level with them. Jonathan had his hands in his pockets and a slight frown between his eyes.

"We'll need more light," he said abruptly. "It's a pity we're using the video camera. It makes everything look too pretty. I hope we can do justice to the stark magnificence of this place. We could have you slowly walking upwards, explaining the purpose of the pyramid as you mount to the resting place of the god. What d'you think?"

"Whatever you say."

"He was a god, wasn't he?"

Lucy nodded, wondering what he was so angry about.

"I've had enough!" Faye exclaimed, breaking her train of thought. "I'm exhausted! I'm going back to Cairo for lunch and a good lie down this afternoon. I would have liked to have seen the Sphinx, but Jonathan says he's busy," she added.

"We could walk down to the Sphinx," Lucy suggested. "I can show you the site of the sacred boat on the way—"

"No, thank you!" Faye sprang back to life. "It's kind of you, Lucy, but I don't want to be told any more about your ancients! To tell you the truth I don't much care for the moderns either. Nor do I ever want to see another temple, especially not if they include mummified crocodiles, or some other horror to give me nightmares."

Lucy was shocked. "Didn't you like anything about your trip?" she asked.

Her sister sighed. "I only came because I thought I'd have Seb to myself for a while and could work on him without any distractions, but he had other things on his mind and I don't suppose we'll ever get together again now. Frankly, darling, I live in this century and it's the only one that interests me. I'm not like you, nor do I want to be. The dead are dead and that's all there is to it. Neither Seb nor I enjoy these smelly old mummies, no matter how grand the surroundings."

"So I've noticed," Lucy couldn't help remarking.

"So take me back to the boat, will you? I'll telephone you, or visit before I go back to England. I can't leave right now anyway because Seb has my ticket with him. It'll be interesting to see how long it'll be before he remembers my existence, won't it?"

They walked out into the bright sunshine in silence. The usual crowd of boys surrounded them until Lucy told them in their own language to go away, which surprised them sufficiently to go and look for easier prey.

Jonathan seemed as glad as Faye to be leaving

the pyramids behind them. He folded Faye solici-
tously into the front passenger seat, leaving Lucy
to get in the back on her own. He didn't even look
at her when she slammed the door shut with such
vigor that the car rocked with its force.

"I shan't be a minute," he said over his shoulder when they arrived at Faye's floating hotel.

Lucy said nothing. There was nothing to say.
She kept telling herself that she had no reason to
feel upset about anything that Jonathan did, but
the serpent of jealousy within her refused to back
down now that it had woken from its previous
slumber. She was fuming by the time he came
back to the car and climbed back into the driving
seat.

He made no comment on her refusal to change
her seat, but drove off in a cloud of dust as if he'd
been driving through the narrow, suicidal streets
of the city all his life.

"Cheer up, Lucy, they have a few more days of
their holiday to go. Seb may be back tonight.
He'll hardly abandon her in Egypt. She'll call you
if she's really in need. Don't worry about her."

"I can't help it," Lucy answered. "What if Seb
doesn't come back?"

"Is he given to walking off?"

"I don't know." Come to think of it, Lucy
knew mighty little about her sister's marriage.
She had always had other things to think about. "I
believe he went off for a couple of days once
before."

"He'll be back."

He drove up to the hotel and got out of the car, leaning over her open window to speak to her more easily. "I'll be back this evening," he told her. "I have a fancy for strolling along beside the Nile at sunset. Will you come with me?"

"If you like," she said offhandedly. She ought to have refused him, she chided herself. But the temptation was too strong.

"Good. I'll see you then."

It was a painful afternoon for Lucy. She tried to work, but Jonathan's image kept getting in her way. She thought how her pulses leapt at the sight of him and, honesty forced her to admit, that what she felt about him was something new to her and not as unwelcome as it should have been. She never had felt for Miles anything like this dissolving warmth and need that Jonathan aroused in her by a look, or a touch of his hand.

Still, she wasn't prepared to risk his contempt when he found out that she was essentially cold and unloving, as Miles had so often told her. Her experience with Miles had been bad enough, with Jonathan it would be devastating. No, if she wanted to stay a part of the human race, she couldn't go walking at sunset with Jonathan Naseby—because she knew that wasn't where it would end. They would both want more, and more, and then the inevitable anticlimax would be that much harder to bear.

Yet she found herself getting ready for him just the same, dressing with enormous care as if he were taking her to a stylish restaurant instead of a walk along a dusty track.

She was delighted she had done so when she went out to greet Jonathan. His first unguarded reaction had been favorable. She could tell, though he had said nothing. The admiring look in his eyes had been enough.

"I thought we might go back to my hotel to eat afterwards," he suggested.

"No, not tonight," she answered quickly.

"What's wrong with tonight?"

"I'm busy tonight," she said.

She knew from the quick, penetrating look he gave her that he wasn't taken in. "Perhaps you'll feel differently after our walk," he said.

"No. No, I won't."

He shrugged his shoulders, drawing her attention to their width and the way the muscles rippled up and down his back when he moved.

She wished she hadn't agreed to go anywhere with him. She felt weak at the knees and quite unlike her usual self.

"You're Miles's widow, not his wife," Jonathan reminded her suddenly.

She turned wide eyes on him. "I know that!"

"Do you?" The open doubt in his voice brought the colour winging up into her face. "Then what's the problem?"

"I told you before," she muttered, "I don't

believe in mixing my work with personal relationships—not the kind you have in mind! If you're lonely in Egypt, I'm sure there are any number of other females who would be only too willing to oblige you."

"True. Perhaps I should've taken Faye up on her offer?"

"I'm not her keeper," she said stiffly.

Jonathan came to an abrupt stop. He put his hands on her shoulders as if he were about to shake her. Then, as suddenly, his expression softened, and he smiled.

"What are we fighting about, Lucy? I don't want Faye, or anyone else at the moment except you, and I know that you want me, too. So what are we waiting for?"

"You don't know what you're talking about!" she shot back wildly. "I'm happy as I am—"

He put a finger across her lips, cutting her off midstream. "Would I have liked Miles?" he asked her.

She shook her head.

"Tell me about him," Jonathan coaxed her.

"There's nothing to tell." The weariness of her tones brought home to her the hopelessness of pretending that she might have changed in the last few years. The memory of what she had experienced with Miles still had the ability to put her teeth on edge, and that had been her fault. There had been any number of other women who had been only too able to satisfy him. It had only been she, his wife, who had frozen up whenever he had come near her after that first, painful time. You'd have thought she would have learned her lesson. Did she want to disgust Jonathan in the same way?

"Nothing?" he said, so gently that the tears came rushing into her eyes.

She sighed. "It was my fault. We only persevered because I wanted children. Miles didn't. In the end he didn't want me either."

Jonathan cupped her chin in his hand, forcing her to meet his gaze.

"It won't be like that with me, Lucy—"

She was shaking. "You don't understand!"

"Oh yes, I do." His tone was grim. "I'm not Miles, however, and I'm prepared to wait until you get that fact through your head. Understand?"

She didn't know if she did or not. She didn't know anything anymore. It was bliss though when his lips took possession of hers and there was nothing in the whole, wide world but the taste and feel of him. His male scent filled her nostrils as his tongue filled her mouth in search of hers. For a long, breathless moment, he was the only reality in her world.

Chapter Five

It didn't take Lucy long to wonder if a few days on her own was a good thing. She had never had the time or the inclination to kick up her heels and take life as it came before, but she was tempted now and it simply wouldn't do! The only thing to do, she determined, was to keep busy. Busy, busy, busy! Then there would be no time to mix business with pleasure or anything else. That had always been her way to escape impossible situations and she was sure it would work for her now—just as long as she stayed away from Jonathan Naseby.

It was this good resolution that took her to Saqqara. Saqqara had always been one of her favourite places. It was redolent with the beginnings of what had probably been the first nation-state in history.

She drove herself there, notebook in hand, but she didn't do much work. She sat on the rough sand, glorying in the endless sunshine and allowing the atmosphere to seep into her bones. With so much history all about her, what did her small concerns matter?

"Hi, there!"

Lucy nearly jumped out of her skin. How had he found her? She had told no one where she was going.

"Hi, there, yourself!" she retorted, sounding anything but pleased.

"I thought you might like to know that I put in a few calls to London last night—"

"Well done!"

Jonathan preened himself, knowing her congratulations to be well deserved. Anyone who takes on the Egyptian telephone system and wins has every right to be pleased with himself.

He sat down beside her. "There's been a small change of plan, but otherwise everything's going better than I thought."

She raised her brows in mute inquiry. There was no doubt about it, Jonathan was looking very pleased with himself indeed.

"A new secretary is coming at the same time as the rest of the team. The good news is that I'm going to direct as well as produce the series. I'd hoped for that all along. I didn't think I'd get both jobs, though, because usually it's against company policy on anything like this. They like to spread the responsibility for success or failure, as the case may be. However, there isn't anyone free who knows the first thing about Ancient Egypt and I managed to persuade them that we have a good rapport going between us and that you'd sooner have me than anyone else."

"Did you, now?" said Lucy.

"A very good rapport," he repeated, taking pleasure in the words as he spoke them.

"I came here to be alone," Lucy said. "There won't be a series at all if you don't give me time to work on the scripts." She waved a hand round the monuments. "It all began here. This must be one of the most exciting places on earth to anyone who has any interest in the past. I want to do it justice."

"Fair enough," he commented. "Tell me about the place and that will fix what you want to say in your mind."

It was the last thing she wanted to do. She could begin by telling him all about Osiris and how he had become the god of the dead, and about the dreaded day of judgment that every soul had to face; it was another matter to concentrate on the matter in hand when he looked at her in that particular way. He had no right to be so very much of a man. She didn't need a man! She didn't need the hassle, and she didn't need the distraction of the small things about him that she couldn't remember even noticing about any other man. Miles, she had worshipped when she had first known him, but she had never noticed the male smell of him, or the way his hair grew out of his scalp, or even the small details of how he cut his nails. She couldn't remember wanting him to touch her as she did this man. It was hopeless! How could she concentrate on her work with him around?

"What do you want to know about Osiris?" she asked him, suppressing her impatience with herself.

"He had something to do with the cult of the dead, didn't he?"

She nodded. "Supreme among the gods was the sun god Re, or Ra, frequently known as Amon-Re. Osiris was his son and ruled over the world until he was murdered by his brother Seth, the god of darkness. His body was cut up in pieces and spread all through the Two Lands. Isis, his sister and his wife, goddess of heaven and earth, searched frantically until she found the severed pieces, which she stitched together. Then she mummified the reunited corpse, whereupon Osiris, whose previous function was no longer open to him, became the god and judge of the dead. It became an art in itself to prepare for judgment, and a whole book was written on the subject, known as the Book of the Dead. There's a very good version on the walls of the *mastaba* of Ti over there—"

"*Mastaba?*"

"It's Arabic for a kind of form that you sit on. The early tombs are shaped the same way, hence the name. That's another thing about Saqqara, you can see the progression from the first tombs to the later, much more sophisticated pyramids. The first pyramid was built in steps, one *mastaba* over another. You can see it over there."

She glanced at him to see if he was taking in what she was telling him, to see that he was frowning down at the ground and not looking at where she was pointing at all.

"Don't make it too heavy, will you?" he warned her.

"I hope not," she retorted. "That's why I need time to work it out and to decide how best to illustrate what I'm talking about. Why don't you go away and leave me to it?"

"I can't," he answered simply. "You may know what you're doing when it comes to the substance, my love, but you're in way over your head when it comes to the pictures. That's what you have a director for. I'm here to work out the camera shots and to keep the cost down. We have to work together or it won't work at all."

"I can't concentrate with you around."

His eyes brightened. "You'll find a way. We don't have to work all the time."

"That's where you're wrong," Lucy said tartly. "I don't like to be distracted when I'm working. It's important to me to make a success of this series and I'm not going to spoil it for myself by playing games with you."

He spread his hands in what could have been surrender. "I hadn't realised we were playing games," he said.

"Hadn't you?" She sounded bitter and wished the words unsaid. It would be just as bad to be fighting with him all the time as it would be to give in to the undoubted physical attraction he held for her.

She looked away. "Perhaps I'm making too much of it," she muttered.

"Perhaps you are," he agreed.

"On the other hand," she continued more calmly, "it's better we should understand each other. Some things are better talked out." She bit her lip, wondering what to say next. She didn't really think that such things should be discussed at all—or even thought about much. She had done very well so far by putting all thoughts of men right out of her mind. The trouble was that Jonathan had a way of inserting himself into her mind when she least expected it, and her defenses against the intrusion were considerably battered because she *liked* Jonathan, she liked him more than she had anyone else for a long, long time. No, perhaps like wasn't the right word either, though she wasn't sure what was.

"You don't understand," she ended feebly, despising herself. She sighed heavily. "This project isn't as important to you as it is to me."

His smile was wry. "Think not? I have a living to earn, too."

She looked at him, shocked, her full attention riveted on him. "I'm sorry," she said finally. "I suppose I was confusing you with somebody else. He was never vulnerable in the ways that I am. He never thought anything could go wrong with anything he chose to do."

"Miles, I suppose?"

She nodded. "I'm apt to judge all men by Miles."

He raised his brows in a silent, mocking comment. "At least your honesty of mind seems unimpaired. To diagnose a problem correctly is halfway to solving it, don't you think?"

"Most men would be proud to be compared to Miles!"

"Now, I wonder whatever gave you that idea?" His arm slipped about her shoulders. "I don't think your erstwhile husband and I would have had much in common."

"Nothing at all," she agreed.

"I can think of one thing."

"Oh?"

She should have seen it coming. She remembered the eagerness with which she had helped to smother the single word, *you,* which had been on his lips. Oh, yes, she had wanted him to kiss her again. She had wanted it all along. But it wouldn't do. Somehow she had to persuade him of that.

"Please don't," she said with dignity.

"No?"

She was distressed to find he was laughing at her. It made her realise as nothing else could how vulnerable she was. She would be a fool to jeopardise all she had going for her for a few kisses from a man who thought she was funny— who probably thought her pathetic as well, if the truth be known. Men did think that women who couldn't hold on to their men were pathetic.

"What do you want from me?" she asked on a sigh.

"It's too soon to tell you that."

She slanted him a look.

"I'm waiting for you to get over the shock of discovering you're as human as the rest of us, no more than that," he finally said.

She looked down her nose. "I don't know what you mean!"

He ran a finger down the straight line of her nose, igniting a flare of awareness that spread through her body with a speed that was almost painful in its intensity.

"If you weren't in a state of shock, my love, I'd take you back to my hotel and let you take your chances on finding out you're glad to be alive after all—"

"I'm not in a state of shock!"

His eyes looked deep into hers. "Is that an invitation?"

"Certainly not!"

She thought her denial sounded prudish and not particularly convincing. Could Jonathan tell it had been a long, long time since any man had meant anything more to her than being just another colleague, or an acquaintance? She rather hoped not.

"It won't commit you to anything to watch the sunset with me and then come home for dinner," he said.

Surely not. She had to have more strength of mind than that. Her marriage must have taught her something, she reasoned, but nothing seemed to have prepared her for the ache of need, the strong desire to reach out and touch where she had no right to touch. She had never much wanted to touch Miles, not after those first few days of disillusionment. It would probably be just the same with Jonathan, she told herself fiercely, and wondered why that should hurt more than anything else.

"The sunset," she said vaguely.

"Haven't you noticed that time has moved on and we're about to witness one of the most splendid sights of the desert?"

"No, I hadn't," she admitted.

"Cheer up, I won't bite," he mocked her, reaching out for her hand to pull her up onto her feet.

"That isn't what I'm afraid of," she said, an ironic twist to her lips.

"Quite right, my dear," he commended her. "You're not afraid of me at all. It's yourself you're afraid of."

"You can't know that!" she rebuked him sharply, and wondered why he laughed again.

"One of these days you're going to be a woman!" He hugged her close up against his warm, hard body. "One of these days—"

Jonathan's room was as empty as only an uninhabited hotel room can be. There were no personal items lying about, nothing to make it his. The sheets were newly laundered and straight from the iron.

"I'm using another room as my office," Jonathan broke in on her thoughts. "I don't like a lot of clutter about in my bedroom."

"So it seems," Lucy said dryly.

"What does that mean?"

"It doesn't look as if you've been in here at all."

His smile was slow and knowing. "I haven't, not a lot. One of us has to keep the show on the road. I've been working."

"Doing what?" she asked.

"Telephoning home mostly. It took some doing to get their consent to my directing as well as producing. They could be right at that. It takes a lot of patience to get anything done out here."

"But you couldn't resist the challenge?" Lucy put in. She knew all about men meeting every challenge that came their way. It wasn't a trait she could find it in herself to admire.

"I have directed before," he answered her. "Afraid I won't do you justice?"

That thought had occurred to her, too, but she wasn't about to admit it. "I could wish you knew more about the subject—"

"That's your job," he pointed out to her quickly. "If you can explain it to me, the chances are you can explain it to your audience out there. You ought to be glad I don't know too much about it. We'd probably quarrel if I did. There are few people more quarrelsome than experts in any field."

"Speak for yourself!" she retorted.

"Isn't that why you bristle every time I come near you? Because you're afraid I'll tread on your academic toes?" The look he cast her dared her to find another reason for why she was still standing in the doorway, her hands clenched.

"If I'm annoyed," she said in carefully moderated tones, "it's because I don't like being interrupted when I'm working. I've always loved being in Egypt so much that I find it difficult to concentrate on why I'm here. I could sit by the Nile and dream away my days with the greatest of ease, but that won't make us any money, will it?"

"Is that what it's all about?"

No! Making money was a matter of indifference to her as long as she had enough to get by. She was afraid that if she didn't concentrate on her work to the exclusion of all else she would wake up to find she had needs and feelings she had long ago talked herself into thinking she would be better off without. She didn't want to get involved with Jonathan Naseby! She would be the one to get hurt, not he. Men like him, ambitious men who liked challenges in their lives, were never the ones to get hurt by their actions—it was the innocent bystanders who took all the flack. Well, once had been enough for her. She had learned her lesson and she wanted no more of it. She was better off alone.

"As a matter of fact," she said loudly, "I was wondering if we should include a piece about the sacred bulls of Saqqara—what do you think? They could only be told apart from ordinary bulls by their black colouring with a white spot on the forehead, another by the tail, and 'to have the likeness of an eagle on its back, double hairs on its tail and the likeness of a scarab beneath its tongue . . .' It might interest the farmers."

He looked at her almost sadly. "Lucy, you don't have to show off to me," he said gently.

"It's important to me to get it right—"

"If it's important you'll weave it in somehow." He sighed. "Why are they important?"

"Saqqara was the necropolis of Memphis, the first capital of the Two Lands. Egypt was the first nation-state in the world. There has to be a reason for that. The bulls, and the gods they represent, made that possible by obligingly arranging themselves into some kind of a hierarchy. Later on, during the Great Heresy of Akhenaton, they even glimpsed monotheism. Much of the

way we organise ourselves today dates back to
Ancient Egypt—"

"Even when it comes to religion?"

"Sure. The Hebrews learned a lot from the
Egyptians and we learned a lot from the Jews."

"The Psalms?"

"You should read the Songs of Akhenaton
sometime."

"Okay, you have me convinced. What place
have these bulls in all this?"

"That's harder to explain. I'd have to do some
work on it. Have I time?"

"If it's important."

She thought about that. "It might be enough to
say they were sacred to Ptah, the local god. It's
funny to me that most people think Egypt never
changed at all for centuries. There were dramatic
changes, but they came slowly. The Egyptians
could never be brought to believe there was
anything better than what they already had!"

"How about you?"

She blinked, unwilling to return to personal
matters. She was more than ever conscious of
being in his bedroom with him. She gave him a
flustered look, wondering if she dared retreat into
history once again. Somehow, she didn't think he
would let her get away with that tactic twice.
There was a determined look about him she
didn't care for.

"What d'you mean?"

"My dear girl, what should I mean? Are you

always going to be content to live with the memory of nothing more than a half-baked love affair for the rest of your life? Is that going to be enough for you? Don't you ever dream of something better than what Miles gave you?"

"Miles was my husband, not my—" She broke off, appalled by what she had almost said.

"Lover," he completed for her, with such satisfaction that she was hard put to it not to reach out a punishing hand and wipe the smile from his face. "You can say that again!"

"I didn't say it at all!" she reminded him.

"You were going to, though, weren't you?"

"I wasn't going to say anything of the sort," she said tartly. "What I was going to say was that our alliance wasn't in any way illicit—it wasn't a half-baked love affair by any stretch of the imagination. It was a full-blown marriage."

"Was that all he left you to hang on to?"

"I have my memories!"

"My love, what memories? Even the most moral, staid marriage can be fun. It doesn't have to be something you'd so much sooner forget that you have to put your feelings into cold storage for the rest of your life."

"I suppose you think the answer to my problems is to have a hectic affair with you?"

"Not yet, perhaps not ever. I don't have affairs with frightened little virgins."

"A widow can scarcely be classed as a virgin!"

she pointed out with asperity, more hurt than she liked to admit to herself.

"A widow with a virgin heart?"

Was that meant to be a romantic description of her state of mind? It sounded to her more like an insult. He thought her a fool, that much was clear, a cowardly fool at that. Perhaps he didn't think she was woman enough to conduct a love affair? If that were the case she'd show him! Oh, it would be a delight to show him the kind of woman she was!

"Why don't you try me and find out?" she asked, sitting down on the edge of the bed, one eyebrow raised in challenge, her gaze unblinking.

He came and stood very close to her, making her look up. She began to wish she hadn't sat down after all, it had put her at a disadvantage. But, come what may, she was *not* going to be the first to look away! She saw the sensuous jut to his lower lip and her heart took off on a race all of its own, refusing to be as calm and dignified as her exterior. She hoped it wasn't panic. This wasn't the moment to take fright at where her own challenge might lead her. Other women did this sort of thing all the time and they were none the worse for it. She might even enjoy it—once she'd got used to it. So what if she hadn't found it any fun in the past? A less selfish lover than Miles might give her some kind of a thrill, and wasn't that what it was all about?

"I wonder if you know what you're doing?" Jonathan murmured.

He still didn't touch her, but just stood, towering above her.

She averted her face, annoyed by the reddening of her cheeks that she knew would betray her. "Is this your idea of making love to a girl?" she asked.

He put a finger under her chin, lifting her face so that she couldn't fail to see the glint of desire in his eyes, nor the determined slant to his mouth. Her breath faltered in the back of her throat.

"Is this what you want?" he breathed against her cheek and then his lips clung to hers, his tongue teasing hers into giving him access to her mouth. It was a kiss like no other that Lucy had ever experienced.

The tension inside her slowly drained. Her fists unclenched, and almost without her being aware, her fingers wound themselves deep into his hair, holding him closer still to her body.

"Yes, this is what I want!" she admitted aloud. "I want you, Jonathan!"

"Mmm," he agreed. It was a satisfactory sound. She wriggled closer still to him. "If you don't stay still," he told her, "you may get more than you bargained for."

It wasn't a warning she was prepared to heed. It was balm to her bruised spirit to know that she could have that effect on him; sheer bliss to know he was having difficulty in controlling himself. It gave her a sense of power that had never come her way before.

"Who's afraid now?" she goaded him.

He released her reluctantly, pushing her back against the bed while he stood up and went over to the other side of the room, leaning his back against the wall, his eyes never leaving her disappointed face.

"I'm not Miles," he said at last. "It seems to me you need some time to do some hard thinking about what you really want, my love. I don't want you to regret anything we might do together—"

"Are you sure it won't be you who'll be having the regrets!" she asked. How could he do this to her?

"Could be," he admitted. "I want to make love to you very much. Perhaps I want to prove to you that you're as desirable a woman as your sister thinks she is." His lips twisted into a wry smile. "Most of all, when I do make love to you, I don't want you to be looking over your shoulder at that dead husband of yours. I want to be the only one in your heart when I make you mine! Prove anything you like to yourself, but don't use me to spite Miles's ghost. If that's all you want a man for, you should have thought of that when he was alive."

Was that what she had been doing? Lucy stared back at Jonathan, not really seeing him at all.

"Miles is the only other man—" she began to defend herself.

He nodded slowly. "Exactly. Tell me when I'm the only man for you and I'll come running. Is it a bargain?"

Her eyes widened in shock. "I can't imagine myself telling you anything of the sort!" she exclaimed.

He walked towards her, pulling her up off the bed to stand beside him. "You'll find a way," he said with confidence.

Chapter Six

Jonathan left her alone for almost a week. Lucy
pretended to herself that she wasn't lonely for his
company. She had never been lonely before when
she'd been staying with Suleiman and his family;
why, she reasoned, should she be lonely now?
She was fortunate that the discipline she had
imposed on herself in the last few years stood her
in good stead now and she was working well. She
had roughed out all the local scripts she thought
she would need. All she needed to do now was to
check up on the details and then get together with
Jonathan to see how they would have to be
amended to suit the camera angles. There were
some things she wasn't prepared to leave out and
he'd have difficulty in getting her to compromise
over quite a bit more, but she was realistic enough
to know that television made its own rules and if a
certain line didn't make a good picture, out it
would have to come.

She was up early, as she always was in Egypt,

for the early mornings were by far the best times of the day. Seated in the same spot where Jonathan had first found her, she frowned over the script she had written illustrating the Great Pyramids of Giza. It was hard to do justice to the last of the Seven Wonders of the Ancient World to still be in existence.

So intent was she on what she was doing that she didn't hear the man on the camel as he came towards her. They were almost on top of her before she looked up and saw them, leaping out of the way, scattering her papers as she did so.

"Look what you've done now!" she said, trying not to look as happy as she felt at seeing Jonathan again. He looked magnificent on the animal, not a bit like the amateur he had to be, she thought.

"Come for a ride with me," he coaxed her. "The crew will be arriving tomorrow or the next day and then we won't have a moment to ourselves."

She squinted up at him. "I thought you were avoiding me," she said.

"I was giving you time to think—"

"Thanks a lot!"

His smile was mocking; his eyes the colour of the river beside them. "Missed me?" he taunted.

She shrugged, avoiding his glance by the simple expedient of picking up the papers she had sent flying and restoring them to order. "Egypt is my second home. Why should I have missed you?"

"Didn't you?"

"I had other things on my mind."

"Like what?"

"Like work," she said. "Why don't you try it sometime?"

He didn't reply. When she cast him a covert glance he was looking far away into the distance. She frowned, annoyed that her barb should have missed.

"Jonathan!"

He had caught her off balance. One moment she was standing on the banks of the Nile, the next she had been scooped up into the air and was perched up before him on the camel, her papers still clutched in her fist.

"Where are we going?" she demanded.

"Where would you like to go?"

She pressed her mouth shut tight, determined not to answer. He took the papers she'd been working on and folded them in a cavalier manner, putting them away in his breast pocket.

"If I go anywhere, I want to go to Giza," she told him through clenched teeth. "If you'd been around, I could have shown you the script and you could've checked it with me to see how it fits in with what you want."

"Okay," he said, "we'll go to Giza."

"By camel?"

"Why not? I'm sure it's one of the usual tourist attractions to ride out to Giza—"

"But not from here! It'll take us all day!"

"Suits me," he said in her ear, "I like the feel of you next to me."

She liked the feeling, too. She didn't need the closeness of his arm about her waist to know the dangers of allowing herself to be carried off by him into the desert. It had an immediate romantic attraction, there was no doubt about that, but was that what she really wanted? She had never thought of herself as the romantic type, riding into the sunset—or in this case the sunrise—with any man.

"If we go, we'll go in a car," she said aloud. "If you must ride a camel, you can hire one by the hotel and ride round the pyramids on it. How's that?"

"One camel between the two of us?"

"I prefer to be in control of my own camel," she asserted. She had always loved the swaying motion of the camel and had taken a delight as a child in riding races with the local children, often managing to come out the winner.

"That figures," he said. "Not giving an inch, are you?"

She could feel his breath moving her hair and she badly wanted to turn her head and let their lips meet. Aloud, she said, "I don't know what you're talking about. Do you want to go to Giza or not?"

"I do." He was laughing at her and she could feel the warm colour come rushing up her neck

and into her face. "And you're not as indifferent
as you like to pretend," he added.

"All I want to do is to get down to some real
work," she said stubbornly.

He set the camel walking in the direction of
Suleiman's house. The motion further under-
mined her resolution to be distant and business-
like where he was concerned. She wanted to look
back and see what he was thinking and feeling. It
wasn't enough to be perched up in front of him
with only the camel's twitching ears in her sights.

"Isn't that what you want?" she asked at last.

"It looks as though it's all I'm going to get right
now," he said mildly. "You're still as tight as a
drum, but watch out, one of these days I'll learn
to play you."

"I prefer to be in charge of my own rhythm, if
you don't mind?"

His fingers touched the nape of her neck. "You
can play your fantasies out on me any time," he
invited her.

But Lucy didn't want to admit she had ever
entertained such notions. She shook her head to
rid herself of the temptation of his touch and
straightened her back just to show him that it
meant less than nothing to her to lean back
against his warmth. If she was careful, she told
herself, he'd never know how close she was to
succumbing to him. Why shouldn't she have an
affair with him? Whom else would she be hurting
besides herself?

It was a relief when they reached Suleiman's house, and taking her by the hands, he swung her down off the camel's back to the ground. He followed more slowly, the camel groaning a protest as she lowered herself to the ground, bit by bit in the curious rocking motion that is unique to the beast.

Jonathan gestured to a small boy who leaped up on its back and went off on the camel along the path they had just traveled.

"Where did you find him?" Lucy asked. She found she felt quite touchy on the subject. Egypt was her pitch and he had no right to be so much at home on her territory. Worse, she wasn't at all sure that she could summon up a camel at will. She could ask Suleiman to hire one for her, but Jonathan wasn't supposed to have these advantages.

"It came my way," he responded. He looked amused and she felt crosser than ever.

She was being ridiculous and she knew it. She'd have her revenge at Giza. If there was one thing she knew about, it was pyramids. She could be really impressive on pyramids! It would be good to be back in the driver's seat.

The guides who stood outside the pyramids waiting for the unwary tourist recognised Lucy from previous encounters with her. Lucy greeted them in Arabic, laughing as they volunteered to take Jonathan off her hands.

"He's with me!" she protested.

"He has his eye on you," one told her teasingly. "You'd better look out. Why not leave him to us?"

"Would you believe we're working?"

"Working!" he scoffed. "Since when has it been work for you to visit the pyramids?"

She told them about the television series and was practically mobbed as they all demanded to be included in some way or another. Most of them could speak a little English and she introduced Jonathan to them, amused that with all the cameras that came to the pyramids and all the VIPs who hung on their every word, they could still be proud and excited that yet another team was going to record their place of work, for that was all it was in the last resort for many of them.

"May we go inside?" she asked them. It was a courtesy request, one they appreciated. Lucy had never put on airs with her learning.

"Of course, madam. Let me check the lights first. We're having trouble with the electricity this morning."

There was the familiar feeling of entering another dimension as she led the way into the largest of the three main pyramids. It was impossible not to be aware of the great mass of stone above their heads, of the sheer solidity of the mass of the building. Lucy turned her head to make sure that Jonathan was close behind her; he was, closer than she liked.

"This is where I want to begin with the pyramids," she told him, her voice breaking unnaturally as she felt his breath stirring her hair. She cleared her throat. "This is the Grand Gallery. It's all of seventy metres up to the top. We're going up there."

Jonathan looked about him. "If you're going to talk in here, you might do better to be coming down the steps rather than going up. How fit are you?"

"Fit enough," she said.

She opened her mouth and began to speak as she climbed ever upwards, explaining that this was the Great Pyramid, the burial tomb of Khufu, in Greek, Keops or Cheops. It is the apogee of the pyramids of Egypt, grander and larger than any of the others, built to maintain and honour the Pharoah in the next life as he had been in this. When it had been opened in modern times, however, there had been little to show what it had been like at the time of the great king's burial. Tomb robbers had taken everything except the great, broken sarcophagus still to be seen in the King's Chamber at the top of the Gallery.

Lucy paced her footsteps so that she arrived at the last, deeper step at exactly the right moment. She turned to Jonathan in triumph.

"What d'you think?" she demanded.

He was leaning against the wall, his arms crossed in front of him, watching her every movement.

"I'm sorry," he said. "With me, it's the singer not the song that I was listening to."

"You weren't listening?" she asked, slightly hurt.

"Not really. Did I miss anything important?"

Lucy told herself she'd do better to laugh it off and tell him it didn't matter to her one way or the other. Her mouth went dry as she looked down on him, as aware of his shadow as she was of the man. She could be swallowed up by him and never see the light of day again, she thought. Her skin prickled with an anticipation that dismayed her. Why didn't she hurry away from him into the King's Chamber? Her feet were weighted as if with lead and she went on staring at him.

It came as no surprise when the lights failed. She stood stock still in the all-pervasive blackness, the scent of centuries in her nostrils.

"There's no need to be afraid," Jonathan whispered against her cheek.

She was torn between joy at the feel of him close beside her and a despairing giggle that he should imagine that she would be afraid of the dark.

"This is my home ground," she reminded him. "Remember?"

"I haven't forgotten. But with all that weight over your head, you could be forgiven a twinge or two of panic."

"How about you?" she challenged him.

He laughed softly. "It seemed a good opportunity to remind you of the differences between us, not the similarities!"

"What differences?" There was a tremor in her voice she struggled to suppress. Could he guess that it was not fear, but rather the excitement she felt in his very masculine presence?

The lights came back on, blinking with the fitful current. Lucy pushed herself away from the man beside her, brushing down her trousers to give herself something to do and to hide her embarrassment at the discovery that she was, after all, as vulnerable to him as any other woman might be. Where was her easy professional manner that she had cultivated so assiduously now?

"Shall we have dinner tonight?" he asked.

"Dinner?" It was impossible to bring her mind to bear on what he was talking about. The planes of his face were accentuated by the dim light and the shadows it cast. It was a strong face, one that was delightful to her. She had a fleeting impression of what it would be like to awaken and find that face on the pillow beside her.

His forefinger caressed the palm of her hand. She snatched it away from him. "I don't know about dinner." She hoped she didn't sound as flustered as she sounded to her own ears. "We ought to spend the time working. If the crew really is coming tomorrow, they won't find anything ready for them."

"We have to eat sometime," he pointed out. "We're working now."

"Are we?"

"I think you have the pyramids adequately covered," he said. They stepped up into the King's Chamber. "Is there some way of contrasting what it was like when they buried him with the spartan look of it now?" he asked.

Lucy nodded. "The pyramid was empty when they entered it," she told him. "I expect the tomb robbers stripped it almost immediately. They were very clever. But, fortunately, Khufu's mother, Hetepheres, probably had similar tomb furniture and hers was found in a tomb shaft to the east of the Great Pyramid. We could show some examples of that."

"Right," he agreed. "So what about dinner?"

"What time?" she found herself asking.

"We'll finish here first," he said. "Then I'll give you time to have a wash and brush up before we go into Cairo. Okay?"

"That'll be lovely," she said in spite of herself.

The afternoon went better than she had expected. Once he had got his own way over dinner, Jonathan listened patiently to her ideas of showing off the pyramids to their best advantage. By the time they left Giza she had the satisfaction of achievement; this was one programme that she knew was going to be good. Apart from her own contribution, who could resist the allure of the Sphinx, or the grandeur of the pyramids?

"You're looking pleased with yourself," Jonathan teased her as he dropped her off at the top of the track that led down to Suleiman's house.

"Shouldn't I be?" she asked.

"Because you've kept me in my place all afternoon?"

"That and other things," she said evasively.

He smiled slowly at her, the glint in his eyes plainly visible. "That's all part of my long term strategy."

Lucy didn't deign to reply, but her footsteps were light as she made her way down the track. She could think of worse fates than being captured by Jonathan Naseby. It was a dangerous sport, but one she was beginning to think herself well qualified for. Taming Mr. Naseby was something that appealed to her. What fun it would be to have a man of his quality eating out of her hand, begging for her favours, and letting her know the power of her attraction for him. As long as it didn't get out of hand, she would enjoy it extremely.

Suleiman took one look at her flushed face and beamed at her. "It's easy to see you've enjoyed your day with your man!" he said.

"We're going into Cairo for dinner," Lucy told him.

"That's well. You'll be safe with this man of yours?"

Lucy preferred not to hear the remark as a question. She smiled the smile of her new confidence, making light of Suleiman's look of doubt.

"I shall wait up until you come home," he insisted. "Tell him that, Miss Lucy. He's a good man, but all men are the same when they find themselves alone with a woman who stirs their desires—"

"There's no need for that," Lucy said hastily. "I'm not afraid that Jonathan will get out of line."

Suleiman heaved a sigh. "Not all men are like that husband of yours!"

Lucy gave him a pert look. "You know nothing about Miles—and very little about Jonathan! Englishmen are brought up differently from you Egyptians. Women are the equals of their men in Europe, I'll have you know!"

Suleiman shook his head. "Men are men, Miss Lucy, and you know very little about them—"

"Ours is a business relationship!"

"So you say, Miss Lucy."

Nothing could destroy Lucy's new confidence in herself, however. She changed into a light-green dress in a flimsy man-made fabric. When she looked at herself in the mirror, she thought she had never looked better.

Suleiman was talking to Jonathan when she left her room. Jonathan's quick glance of amusement in her direction told her all too clearly what they had been talking about.

"I'm ready!" she announced.

Jonathan got to his feet immediately. "Very nice, too!" he commented.

Lucy thought he also looked nice, but she didn't say so. He had changed into a pair of fawn trousers, with a cream shirt and jacket. It accentuated the outdoor, tanned look he had acquired. She was tempted to reach out a hand and touch the strong line of his jaw. Oh, dear, she thought, perhaps Suleiman was right to be worried about her after all!

The sky had changed from blue to purple, streaked with gold and green, and finally a crimson that lit up half the sky calling attention to the great scarlet orb that was slowly slipping down the horizon.

The light was rapidly fading as they entered the Cairo traffic jam. As they approached the river the waits grew longer, but neither of them minded. They were just coming up to the statue of Rameses II when the *muezzins* entered their minarets. The musical, plaintiff sound of them calling the faithful to prayer came from all quarters of the city and rose over the sound of the traffic and the street traders calling their wares. It was one of those perfect moments that Lucy knew she would remember all her life.

Chapter Seven

"So," said Jonathan, reaching for her hand across the table. "Tell me about that marriage of yours."

"There's nothing to tell." Lucy refused to meet his eyes. Instead she gazed out at the snowy white tablecloth and the artfully arranged flowers in the centerpiece. "I was married. He was killed. End of story."

"Not quite," Jonathan said. "You flare up whenever the fellow's mentioned. What went wrong?"

"Nothing!" she denied. She thought she did it rather well, opening her eyes wide in innocence and putting a sweet, soft smile on her face that ought to have deceived any man who took the trouble to look. "Or rather, what did wasn't his fault. I knew what he was when I married him."

"Are you implying that you couldn't stand his racing?" Jonathan inquired.

"In a way. I tried it once or twice. A lot of people find motor racing exciting and the men who do it even more so. I nearly died of boredom. Can you believe that? A lot of noisy cars, indistinguishable from one another, roaring round and round in circles. As often as not I didn't even know which one *was* Miles!"

"Okay, so you went back to work during the racing season. What went wrong with the marriage?"

"I was what went wrong. I couldn't fulfill my obligations. It was as simple as that."

Jonathan looked at her, his eyes narrowed. She wished she knew what he was thinking.

"I don't believe that," he said at last. "Oh, I believe that he made you feel something less than a woman because you couldn't have children. Gave you an outsize in inferiority complexes while he was about it. I accept that. He was obviously an insensitive clod who never gave a thought to his partner's needs and wants as long as his own were satisfied. But, knowing you, you wouldn't have let it rest there. You'd have enlisted the medical profession and half the soothsayers of Egypt to help you—if you'd wanted help. Why didn't you?"

"I saw a few doctors."

The remembered humiliations came flooding back. Miles crowing that there was nothing wrong with him! Her own hurt and despair. And perhaps it wouldn't have mattered all that much to her if he hadn't kept harping on her inadequacies. He

had made her doubt her ability to attract any
other man.

"Did Miles?"

Lucy shrugged. "He didn't have to."

"Why not?"

That had been the final humiliation. It was
something she had never even told her family.
She hadn't wanted anyone to know. She didn't
now, so she couldn't understand why she was
about to blurt the whole story out to Jonathan. To
Jonathan of all people, the only man besides
Miles who'd made her want something more than
a casual kiss—

"Miles had already fathered a child," she said.

Jonathan muttered an oath.

"Don't Jonathan! None of it matters now," she
said. "I've grown out of wanting motherhood for
a career. I'm doing very nicely with what I have.
This TV series will mean far more to me than a
child ever could!"

"It shouldn't have to be either/or," Jonathan
said.

"It nearly always is."

Jonathan raised an eyebrow. "Who told you
that? Motherhood doesn't keep women at home
these days."

Lucy swallowed the lump in her throat.
"Wouldn't you expect your wife to stay at home?"

He shook his head.

"Miles wanted his children to be properly cared

for." She tested him: "Young children need their mothers at home."

"Not twenty-four hours a day, they don't. You could do a lot of your work at home anyway. These trips don't come up every day, do they?"

"We weren't talking about me. The question doesn't arise for me."

"It doesn't arise for me either," he pointed out, "yet you were happy enough to talk about what I should want my wife to do."

"I wanted to know." She caught her lower lip between her teeth and fought the embarrassment that threatened to overwhelm her. She was be- having like a daft teenager!

Jonathan chose not to press home his advan- tage. "I'm not Miles," he said. He smiled a long, slow smile that made her heart turn over within her. "Think about it. Some men don't remain boys forever."

If she felt confused as he summoned the waiter and paid for their meal, it was a pleasant confu- sion. She felt really happy and the feeling was such a novel one that she realised she hadn't been happy for a long, long time. She hadn't even been content. She'd killed any feeling she might have had with overwork and had determinedly enjoyed her success, all the time knowing, deep down, that it didn't really matter to her whether she became famous or not.

So what did she want? She looked at the well-muscled lines of Jonathan's back as she followed him out of the restaurant. If things had been different, she thought, she could have wanted him.

The sights and sounds of Cairo were as vivid by night as they were by day. There was never enough space for everyone who wanted to move into the capital. Every day more and more villagers gave up their farms and came to look for work and prosperity in the city. No matter how the authorities tried to supply their needs for housing and everything else, they never caught up with this endless tide of humanity leaving the land in search of sophistication and the urban way of life. The streets were always thronging with people, some of them still herding the animals they had brought with them, not knowing that there would be even less room for their goats, sheep, and their beasts of burden than there was for themselves. The lucky ones had friends or relations already established in some trade who could give them a helping hand. The unlucky ones held on as best they could, only a few giving up altogether and returning to the villages whence they had come.

As Lucy waited for Jonathan to find the car and come back to the door of the restaurant to pick her up, she feasted her eyes on all that was going on around her. Next door was a tourist boat waiting to take a party of travellers the six hundred mile journey up the river to Aswân and the new dam which had raised the water level under the city, flooding the basements of many of the older buildings. On the way they would see unfolded before their eyes the centuries of Pharaonic rule, the many temples that still lay beside the waters of the Nile.

"Ready?" Jonathan called.

She started, knowing she had been deliberately wool-gathering rather than thinking about him.

She quickly got in the car beside him, smoothing her skirts neatly over her knees like a schoolgirl, trying to ignore the eager leap in her blood as her thigh brushed his.

"Isn't the Nile beautiful at night?" she remarked. The comment sounded banal even to her own ears.

"Beautiful!" he agreed. He slowed the car to let her off at the top of the track that led to Suleiman's house.

"It's been a lovely evening," she told him. "Thank you very much for taking me out to dinner—and everything."

He reached out a hand, interrupting her scrabbling for the door handle. "Everything?"

She made the mistake of turning her face towards him. He was waiting for her, his mouth taking possession of hers with an ease that made it seem all the more natural. She made a choking sound of protest at the back of her throat and then she forgot everything else except how nice he tasted and the delightful sensation of his lips against hers. She made a small movement with her hand, seeking the hardness of his shoulders and chest, and uttered a sigh of content as she found the nape of his neck and explored the vigorous growth of his hair just above his collar.

His lips left hers, exploring the line of her jaw and nibbling on the lobe of her ear.

"Come home with me tonight, little Lucy, to my hotel."

She shook her head, "Not tonight," she said.

He released her abruptly. "Are you trying to tell me that Miles still haunts you after all this time?"

Again, she shook her head, shutting her eyes tight because she didn't want to see the contempt he must be feeling for her.

"Take a chance, Lucy, and stay with me!"

For the third time she shook her head. "I can't. We have work to do. Ask me again when the filming is finished."

She slammed the door shut and smiled at him through the glass. He probably couldn't see her, which was just as well, for her smile was decidedly apologetic. She stepped away from the car and followed up the smile with a wave of her hand. She was expecting him to take off with squealing tires and grinding gears, but he slowly eased the car forward.

"Never mind, love," he said through the open window, his voice a caress as it reached her. "My turn is coming. Isn't it?"

She made no answer, pressing her lips tightly together.

"Isn't it, Lucy?" he repeated with a lazy urgency that set her nerves quivering.

"Yes," she managed.

He reached out of his open window and touched her cheek. "That's a promise," he said, before he drove away.

As Lucy walked slowly down the path to Suleiman's house she did her best to persuade herself that if it was a promise at all it was one made under duress, so it didn't count. Yet nothing could quite quell the thrill that passed through her when she thought of Jonathan's kisses. She wished she had had the courage to go to his hotel with him. What harm would it have done? She was answerable to nobody but herself.

Suleiman's courtyard was lit up despite the lateness of the hour. When Lucy paused by the doorway, she saw that he had company. With a sinking heart she recognised the visitor to be Faye. Only bad news could have brought her sister there. Lucy squared her shoulders, took a deep breath, and went inside to greet her.

Sharing a bed with her sister was not Lucy's idea of comfort. In the heat she had revelled in having a double bed to herself; now Faye had two-thirds of it and wanted more and, as if that weren't enough, showed no signs of going to sleep. Instead she was working herself up into a state over Seb's defection.

Lucy tried telling herself she was being selfish.

By three in the morning, however, she no longer cared what she was being. She had had enough. Flouncing over onto her back, she gave up all thought of sleep.

"Okay, so why are you here?"

Faye lit another cigarette. "Meaning you don't want me here, I suppose. You've made that pretty clear. What have you got going on that you don't want me to know about?"

"Nothing."

Here we go again! Lucy thought. Why could her family never leave her alone? Hadn't Faye problems enough of her own?

"Do you have to smoke in bed?" she asked irritably.

"Seb never objects."

Seb wouldn't, Lucy thought. He was a chain smoker himself. Lucy had never smoked, however, and she disliked the smell of nicotine in her bedroom. It was pointless saying anything more, though, that much she knew. Faye thrived on opposition and would only smoke more than ever.

"Where's Seb now?"

To Lucy's dismay her sister burst into tears. "He took off without me. I never thought he'd really leave me. Lucy, what am I going to do without him?"

Lucy didn't reckon her judgment of men to be of much use to anyone, least of all herself. She thought Sebastian would be back after a while, but was there any use in telling Faye that now?

"How long ago did he go?" she asked instead.

"He was on the same flight as that secretary woman of that dishy Jonathan of yours. Now, there's a man I could go for in a big way! What's he like, Lucy?"

"He works hard," Lucy said.

"But does he play hard?"

"I really couldn't tell you."

Faye, her tears forgotten, regarded her sister in amusement. "No, you wouldn't, would you? I don't suppose you ever open your mouth in his presence except to tell him something he doesn't want to know about some ancient god or other. I can't think how you ever persuaded Miles to marry you! You've probably never even noticed Jonathan! You don't mind if I have a go at him, do you?"

"It wouldn't stop you if I did," Lucy retorted. "What about Seb?" she added with a touch of malice. She couldn't help wondering if Faye were really missing her errant husband, or whether the flood of tears hadn't been an act put on for her benefit. It had taken Faye a long time to get upset about her Sebastian's absence if she hadn't said a word to anyone about it for a week.

"What about Seb?" Faye repeated.

"He's been gone a week—"

"I thought he'd come back! This holiday cost a fortune! I didn't think he'd leave in the middle of it! Well, when I thought how much it had cost, I decided to go ahead and enjoy myself without him. It wouldn't have been the first time. Our marriage has always been like that. We agreed right at the beginning that we'd understand if the other one wanted to have a fling from time to time. Seb often did! But he always came back to *me!* Only, this time I don't think he's going to. He was so unkind. Said I'd meant nothing to him for years, that I'd become a tired habit with him, and that this time our marriage wouldn't freshen with a new adventure. What he wanted was a new marriage! I can't bear it, Lucy, I can't, really! I always meant to be the one who walked out on him if we were going to finish things. It's so humiliating to be left in the lurch like this! I'll show him, though! Two can play at his game! I think I'll marry Jonathan and see how Sebastian likes that!"

"Jonathan?" Lucy repeated dumbly. "What will that prove?"

"That I'm still an attractive woman."

Lucy was dismayed to feel a strong urge to wipe the self-satisfied look off her sister's face.

"Jonathan thought so when we met the other day," Faye continued. "You must have noticed, Lucy! I know you never notice anything that didn't happen sometime B.C., but even you must have noticed that!"

Lucy couldn't bring herself to comment. "I'm going to sleep," she announced. "Try not to set the bedclothes on fire, won't you?"

"My word, we smokers are persecuted these

days by you health nuts! Why can't you leave us alone to do our own thing? We don't go on and on to you about not smoking!"

"I'm not sharing your bedroom, you're sharing mine," Lucy pointed out.

"So what? I'm not doing you any harm!"

Lucy gritted her teeth. "Good night," she said.

It was the same at breakfast. Amina was as sulky as Lucy felt, casting black looks in Faye's direction and her lighted cigarette in one hand while she ate with the other. Lucy's patience was severely strained by the end of the meal. She objected to having ash in the milk and, even more, to listening to Faye's disparaging remarks about herself, about Seb, and about her children. Poor little devils, she thought, wondering if either parent ever gave them a thought except when it was convenient to them. If the opportunity came her way, she vowed, she would make it her business to see exactly what kind of a life they were leading. Where were they now while their parents were gadding about making a mess of their own lives?

"I'm sorry I can't spend the morning with you," Lucy said aloud, draining her cup, not in the least bit sorry, "but I have to go over to Jonathan's hotel to see if the crew has arrived. We'll be starting filming soon."

Faye's eyes narrowed. "I'll come with you. I presume Jonathan will be there?"

"He'd better be. We've had enough delays—"

"I got the impression that Jacqueline had mis-understood the position. She was crying when Seb caught his plane to London."

Lucy was surprised. "You were there?"

"Of course I was there. I wanted to make sure he really did go back to England. I wasn't going to tell everyone on the awful boat that he'd been called back home and then have him turn up at the next stop. I can't say I blame him for leaving in a way. You have no idea how earnest everyone was! We had a lecture every evening telling us all—and I mean *all*—that we were going to see the next day. Would you believe some people actually took notes?"

Lucy, who had once been a guest lecturer on one of those boats, sent a silent message of sympathy to her colleague.

"Did you or Seb take in a single word?" she asked.

"My dear, all those temples are exactly the same! See one and you've seen them all."

"Even Luxor?"

Faye shrugged. "I cried off seeing Luxor or Karnak. Why have they two names as they seem to be much the same place? No, don't tell me! That was what Seb and I quarrelled about. He inferred I wasn't taking our reconciliation serious-ly if I could let him go sightseeing on his own. That was what made him take off back to his lady love, promising never to return to me! With Jonathan in the offing, it just could be good riddance, don't you think?''

Lucy didn't, but she knew better than to say as much. "You'll be just as bored talking about our film scripts," she warned.

Faye batted her lashes. "With Jonathan there? You have to be joking!"

Jonathan greeted Lucy and Faye with something approaching enthusiasm.

"They've arrived! A pretty good team—better than I'd expected. We've got everyone I asked for except Larry Norton. He's still tied up on another project, but I gather they're sending him on as soon as he's finished. We can't do better!" He gave Lucy a considering look, lightened by a brief smile. "They must think pretty highly of you to send out all their best men! We're going to be a success, little Lucy! A formidable success! How are you going to enjoy having a famous sister, Faye?"

"It'll be you who'll be making her look good," Faye said rashly.

"We're a team," Jonathan nodded. "But Lucy's fronting the project, and it's her knowledge we're projecting. She's good at it, too! She's got me hooked on Ancient Egypt and we've hardly begun yet."

Faye turned her eyes heavenwards. "Not you, too! Well, I for one prefer to live in the present and enjoy myself while I can. I don't want to think about death. It's morbid to go on and on about things like that."

Lucy was inclined to argue. "But death is a part of life. The Egyptians didn't separate the two. One's apt to think that Ancient Egypt flowered into being all by itself, but a lot of it came up the Nile from the African interior. In fact, many of the Pharoahs were black men."

"Is that so?" Jonathan asked with interest.

"Don't!" Faye groaned. "Once she gets started, nothing will stop her!"

"You shouldn't have come with her," Jonathan told her. "Why did you?"

"To see you, of course."

Jonathan's shrewd eyes lingered briefly on Lucy. "It's obvious you didn't get much sleep last night," he said. "Was there a good reason for that?"

"The best," she answered abruptly. "I hate sharing a bed, especially with someone like Faye who wants all the bed and talks all night long, not to mention smoking all through the small hours."

"Poor Miles!" said Faye, with a shake of her head.

Lucy blenched.

"I don't think I'd have cared for Miles much," Jonathan observed.

"You mustn't believe all that Lucy has told you about him," Faye said pertly.

"She's said very little."

"Miles was a hero to us all," Faye said. "Lucy couldn't live up to him, that's all."

Lucy would have preferred not to have to listen to any more. She tried to change the conversation. "When am I going to meet the crew?" she asked. She might just as well not have spoken at all.

"I don't know what you mean," Jonathan said, his attention wholly on Faye. "Did Miles ever grow up?"

"No, I can't say he ever did," Faye answered. "But that was Lucy's fault. She couldn't give him what he wanted."

Jonathan's mouth tightened into a bleak line. Lucy knew exactly what he was thinking and none of it would be to her credit.

"Did he know what he wanted?" he asked.

Faye laughed, opening her eyes wide as she gazed back at Jonathan. Slowly she licked her lips with the tip of her tongue. "You've got to be joking!" she exclaimed. "But it doesn't matter what the man wants in the end, does it? It's what the woman decides she wants that counts. That's where poor Lucy fell flat on her face. She thought Miles was in love with her when anyone with half an eye could have seen he was so much in love with himself there simply wasn't room for anyone else."

Lucy curled up inside, wishing she were dead.

"Poor Lucy indeed," said Jonathan with feeling.

Chapter Eight

The filming was going well. Lucy had seen some of the footage and had been fascinated by the way her own image had come over as a quiet, serious girl with a look of haunting beauty she had never seen in her mirror.

"But I'm not at all like that!" she'd complained to Jonathan.

"Video cameras always prettify everything," he'd told her without the glimmer of a smile.

She had given him look for look, trying to see him through Faye's eyes. She did that constantly now. As with an old wound, she couldn't resist nagging at it, to see if it still hurt. More and more, when the two of them were together, Lucy felt like the fifth wheel on the coach. They talked together, laughed together, and if Faye was to be believed, did a great deal more than that together.

Lucy tried to persuade herself that what they did made no difference to her, but for the first time in her life she knew what it was to be jealous and she was ashamed of herself. She couldn't remember, even in those first heady days of marriage with Miles, that she had ever felt the barbs of naked jealousy before. She had been hurt when Miles had gone off with other women, but now she knew it was her pride that had been hurt and not herself as a person.

At least it wasn't affecting her work. There she had never done better. She was particularly pleased with the scene she had dreamed up for the day's filming. It was the episode she wanted to show first, to show how the Egyptians had conducted their lives so many centuries before. They had already taken shots of her in various tombs, pointing out the little scenes taken from life that she now hoped to realise by holding a similar party in Suleiman's patio.

Looking round, she was well satisfied with what she saw. Christopher Moss, the floor manager, caught her eye and grinned at her. Jonathan might have been more and more aloof these last two weeks, but she got on well with the rest of the crew.

"I think we're about ready," he said. He was the only one of them who spoke Arabic fluently and he had done wonders, gathering up the villagers under Suleiman's supervision to take the part of the guests at the feast.

Paddy O'Rourke and Jim O'Reilly, the two camera men, known as the Irish twins, consulted with each other over their marked scripts, making sure they had their angles right. Only Jonathan was missing and Lucy had no doubt at all that he was lingering for a last few minutes with Faye.

Judy, the script supervisor, cast an impatient glance around. "Where is he?" she mouthed above the din.

Lucy shrugged her shoulders. The final humiliation would be to have anyone know how much she cared. She couldn't help, however, sighing a sigh of relief when he appeared in the doorway alone, seeking her out with his eyes.

"Ready to roll?"

He made it sound like an intimate question for her alone. Lucy took a last glimpse at her amended script and nodded her head. This was the part of the proceedings she most enjoyed, which had been an unexpected bonus, for she had thought she would be shy before the cameras. She had done all the hard work, had made the script as good as she possibly could, and now she was committed to translating it into reality, making it come alive for all the viewers who would see it on the television in the future.

It was easy to transmit her own liking for these ancient people. They had been excellent trenchermen, she pointed out. Indeed, their standard of living had probably been higher then than it was now for the people who dwelt beside the Nile. She moved towards a table set out with the main fruits and vegetables that had been known to the

Ancient Egyptians. There were figs, dates, apples, pomegranates, and the occasional coconut by way of luxury. Oranges, lemons, peaches, pears, cherries, and bananas were not yet known. By way of vegetables, there was a plentiful supply of onions, leeks, beans, garlic, lentils, chick-peas, spinach, turnips, radishes, and fantastic lettuces, just as there are today. Lettuce was served with oil, vinegar, and salt, not a French dressing at all, but an Ancient Egyptian one. There were also cucumbers, any number of gourds, melons, and pumpkins. Edible oils, she explained, were supplied from the *bak* tree until the advent of the olive tree sometime in the later dynasties. Castor oil was used both for medicinal purposes and for lighting the many lamps that were necessary to light the large rooms in which they lived.

She was able to show a variety of the lamps that had been found in various tombs over the years. They differed in design and decoration, but all of them worked on the same principle as the storm lamp does today. Some of them gave out a pretty good light, though the degrees of heat they added to the atmosphere must have been unwelcome in the hot months of summer.

The staple diet of the Egyptians had been meat. Here there was a welcome break in the proceedings as everyone relaxed while Judy wrote in the various shots they had already taken illustrating how the beef had been specially fattened for slaughter, the fillet regarded as the choicest cut exactly as it is today. There were illustrations, too, of sheep and goats and the red-coated mouflon, and even more of the vast wild-fowl industry based in the marshlands of the Delta. It had been quite hard to select the best and the most colourful of these scenes. Because they had had little to do with religion, the artists had really been able to let themselves go and there were a series of delightful ducks and other fowl, some of them caught from the most amusing angles.

Many of the Pharoahs had been huntsmen and had often been represented in the chase, hunting venison from the oryx, gazelle, and ibex, all of which had been readily available in those days.

"It's going well," Judy told Lucy. "What do you want to take next? Your talk on fish, or the sequences of the party?"

"How ready is everyone?"

"Chris is still coaching some of them in what they have to do."

"Okay, then let's get rid of the fish, shall we?"

"Don't you like fish?"

Lucy relaxed into laughter. Judy had a happy knack of putting her at her ease whenever she tightened up and looked like making a mess of things.

"Fish was a very dangerous commodity! It was sacred to the malignant brother Seth, he who murdered Osiris in a fit of jealousy. It was subject to any number of taboos. I can't help thinking of them whenever I am served fish."

"Fool," said Judy. "Fish is good for you."

Lucy laughed. "I still have reservations about it," she said.

"I'd noticed. You never order fish when we all eat together at the hotel. I thought you might have known something we didn't. To go down with a stomach bug while we're here is not my ambition."

"Keep away from raw foods and you'll be all right," Lucy advised.

"I'll remember that," Judy said.

Finally they were ready to film the party scenes. The villagers were giggling awkward in their hastily contrived clothing of fine linen. Lucy helped persuade them that this was what indeed their ancestors had once worn, however, only by the richest in the land. Although they all knew better, none of them were prepared to admit they were descended from anything less than an administrator. Not even the wigs, sweltering in the afternoon heat, could put them off after that. They giggled some more when Judy balanced perfumed lumps of fat on top of their wigs, and they were completely disbelieving when they started to dissolve, giving out a perfume they would really rather have been without. The first scenes showed them drinking wine, which was then confined to the upper classes and was now confined to the Christians, because alcohol is forbidden to Moslems. Beer had been the national drink all those years ago and that was more of a problem, but it looked convincing enough through the eye of the camera and that was all that mattered.

The serving girls came on, bearing trays of milk, butter, cheese, and any number of eggs, though the domestic hen was not yet known. These were offered to the guests as sweetmeats and were eaten accordingly. Everybody began to enter into the spirit of things, trying a bit of this and a bit of that and the party was going well until Jonathan suddenly called a halt to the proceedings.

"Lucy, you never mentioned pork among the meats! Judy, why didn't you call our attention to that? We'll have to go back over it."

"No need," Lucy assured him. "Pork was forbidden then as it is now all over the Middle East. It was always considered unclean."

"It didn't come in with the Jews?" Jonathan ran his fingers through a loose bit of hair. "Are you sure of your facts? Faye—"

"Quite sure," Lucy said coldly.

"Well, you seem definite enough anyway," he muttered.

"What did Faye say?" Lucy demanded sharply.

"Nothing."

"How interesting."

The loose bit of hair became wilder still. "Faye

is going through a bad patch. She was only trying to be helpful."

"How? By interfering in something she knows nothing about?"

"It wasn't that at all. She only said things were going too well and that you only worked at your best when you were challenged a bit. She wants you to be a success—"

"How little you know her."

"Lucy, don't be difficult. Wasn't it true that you lost interest in Miles after he ceased to be a challenge to you? Haven't you lost interest in me?"

"If you care to think so."

"I think she may know you better than I do. She's your sister after all."

"And she wants you for herself."

Lucy was never to know what Jonathan would have answered because Judy came running over to them, a frown crinkling her forehead.

"Jonathan, can we get on with things?" she pleaded with him. "We can't keep these people here forever. We're all set to do the tableau of the party, the host seated on his marble chair. Oh lord, where do the women sit?"

"On the floor, along with the children and the lesser guests," Lucy told her. "The chief male guests sit on the few chairs they had."

Judy cast her a speaking look. "I suppose the women were as usual all second class citizens?"

"Oh, no," Lucy assured her, "they had a power all their own. Property and wealth descended through the woman. Haven't you ever wondered why Cleopatra was such a much married lady?"

"Is this in the script?" Jonathan demanded.

"A later one, when we get farther up the Nile."

"But I want to know now!" Judy protested.

"Cleopatra was the heir to Egypt," Lucy explained hurriedly, a wary eye on Jonathan's face. "Anyone who wanted to be Pharoah had to marry her to get Egypt. She was forced to marry her elder brother, then her younger brother, then Caesar, for even Rome was obliged to follow the much older Egyptian customs. She even married Mark Antony to make his rule of Egypt legal. Only when she was asked to submit to Octavius did she draw the line. She preferred death and consequently clasped the asp to her bosom. I think I would have, too."

Jonathan's eyes narrowed. Lucy was embarrassed to discover that she had his full attention now; Faye was forgotten. "But you didn't, did you?" he said for her alone.

"I did the next best thing," she said. "I buried myself in my work."

Judy's eyebrows rose as she looked from one to the other of them. "I thought Octavius was some kind of pervert?"

"He was," Jonathan confirmed. "They're not confined to ancient times, unfortunately."

"But Lucy was married to Miles Jameson—"
She broke off, covering her mouth with her hand.
"Oops, sorry! Forget I said anything, will you?"

"Don't worry," Lucy reassured her. "Miles was
no pervert. He was everybody's hero."

"Except his wife's?" Jonathan slyly interjected.

"I was the inadequate one," Lucy said abruptly. She turned her attention back to her script
with such determination that no one ventured to
continue the conversation.

Her work that day, however, had lost its power
to soothe and reassure her. Miles might just as
well have been at her elbow, his presence was so
vivid to her: the hurt, dangerous look in his eyes;
and even his naked hatred with which he had
turned away from her the last time she had
begged him to try once again for the child they'd
both longed for.

It was unfortunate that the last sequence of the
day should deal with divorce. The party had been
so much enjoyed by the villagers that they were
still cluttering up Suleiman's house, giving the
perfect background against which Lucy was trying
to speak. It was only when she was well launched
on her lecture about the ease of divorce in
Ancient Egypt that Lucy became aware that Faye
had joined them.

Lucy hated working with a member of her
family present. She could feel herself tightening
up inside, hoping that her tension wouldn't be

picked up by the cameras. Her eyes flickered across the patio to where her sister was standing, and to her dismay, she saw that Faye was crying. The tears were causing her black mascara to run down her cheeks.

"Cut!" Jonathan bit out. "What's the matter now, Lucy?"

"I'm not sure divorce fits in very well with partying—"

"You should have thought of that before. We've been over this script half-a-dozen times and this is the first time you've raised the point. Nobody else had any objection to make."

Lucy looked uneasily at Faye's miserable face. If the mention of divorce could upset her perhaps she really was missing Sebastian more than she cared to admit. Marriage was one play in which the onlooker definitely did not see most of the game.

"Do I have to start at the beginning again?"

Jonathan consulted his script. "I suppose not. Wrap it up and we'll call it a day. Tomorrow we start for Luxor!"

The camera came in close, too close for comfort, while Lucy obediently rehearsed the closing lines of the first programme.

"The important point to remember is that the Ancient Egyptians were people like ourselves; lovable and hateful. By the end of this series, I hope you will have made a voyage of discovery in

time and will have found out how much modern
mankind, especially those of the Western world,
owe to this the first of the great nation-states."

Luxor had always been one of Lucy's favourite
places and not even the prospect of having to
continue to share a room with Faye was able to
depress her spirits as they drove into the little
town and took up residence in one of the leading
hotels overlooking the Nile. From her bedroom,
Lucy could see a felucca preparing to set sail, a
tiny boy climbing up the tall, curving mast to ease
the sail up.

The feluccas were like the spirit of Egypt, Lucy
thought, plying their trade up and down the Nile,
unchanged for how many thousands of years? No
one knew. From the earliest times these graceful
boats had been depicted as being part of the
Egyptian scene.

She was still leaning over the balcony when
Jonathan spied her from below. "I am looking for
you to guide me round the Temples of Karnak,"
he called out to her. "When are you coming
down?"

"Where's Faye?" she called back.

"Temples aren't her scene, remember?"

Lucy hesitated. Did she want to be alone with
him? In a way she did, if only because she always
felt more alive in his company, but in a way she
didn't. Faye would have told him by now all about
her marriage to Miles—from her point of view—

and Lucy knew he would be as contemptuous of her as a wife as her family had been all along. None of them had been able to understand her need to have a career of her own, nor her reasons for refusing to trail round the world behind Miles from one Grand Prix to the next.

"I'll come down," she said.

She didn't want to go to the Temple of Karnak with him, but a previous argument between them came vividly to her mind.

"The Egyptians didn't understand perspective," he had said. "We had to wait for the Greeks to see things as they really are!"

She had denied it hotly, but he hadn't believed her. Now she could prove it to him once and for all.

He was waiting for her at the entrance to the hotel when she got outside. She saw him before he did her and the sight brought a spasm of joy to her that was so intense that she had to stand still for a moment to give herself time to recover her equanimity. His pale green shirt was open almost to the waist, revealing a gold medallion that was much the same colour as his tanned skin. His pale drill trousers looked as if they had been tailored especially for him. It didn't matter that he had his hands in his pockets and was leaning against the wall in the only bit of shade he could find. He looked as much at home there as he would have done in the middle of Piccadilly Circus.

"We're going to the museum!" With head tilted

at an angle the better to look him in the face, she nevertheless had an air of decision about her that plainly amused him.

"Is it relevant?" he asked.

"It is to the argument we were having the other day. Are you coming?"

His smile was slow and intimate. "My dear girl, you ought to know by now that I'd go anywhere with you."

Lucy pretended she hadn't heard him. What could he mean by it? Was it possible that he preferred her to her sister after all? Not according to Faye, but then Faye had never been a reliable source of information.

"If Faye had been around we could have taken her with us," she tested him aloud.

"I shouldn't have thought Faye visited a museum more than once a year," Jonathan commented.

"If that."

"She's jealous of your brains."

"Don't be ridiculous!"

He looked down on her from his superior height, sucking in his cheeks thoughtfully. "Why do you always sell yourself short?" he asked casually.

She was unable to answer. "Most people prefer Faye," she mumbled after a while.

"Did Miles?"

She hunched her shoulders defensively. "He married me," she pointed out.

"So he did. Faye, I gather, wasn't available."

If that was what he wanted to believe, let him! Lucy began to walk fast down the street, uncaring of whether he followed on or not. She was so intent on her own misery that she failed to realise he had summoned up one of the horse-drawn vehicles that abounded outside the hotel until it drew up beside her, the thin, mangy animal panting down the back of her neck as its driver brought it in close.

"It isn't far to the museum!" she protested.

"But it is hot," he pointed out. "Get in, Lucy, and stop playing games." He waited until she had done so and then he went on. "Sooner or later, you're going to have to sort things out with that sister of yours. You tighten up whenever she's around and it shows. Do what you like in your own time; be as much of a martyr as you choose; but in my time, get rid of her! She's ruining your performance."

Lucy looked down and was shattered to discover her hands were shaking. "Why don't you get rid of her?" she suggested. "You don't really want to, do you?"

"I know I'd like to wring her neck for you." He sounded as though he meant it. And he was right. Faye did undermine both her concentration and her confidence in herself, and Jonathan had every right as director to insist that she did something about it. Her heart sank at the prospect. If Faye really wanted to get her teeth into Jonathan it would take more than the persuasion she had at her disposal to change her mind . . .

Lucy knew exactly what she wanted to show Jonathan in the museum. She hurried up the stairs, leading the way to a showcase where a wall had been built. The wall was covered with paintings, so natural that one could reach out and touch them.

"They even painted like this inside the temples," she told Jonathan, "but after Akhenaton's death, they removed every reference to the dead Pharoah, obliterating him from the face of the earth. They changed all the temple paintings, too, changing them back to the old style. You can see the alterations quite clearly in some places. Do you believe me now that the way they represented things had a religious significance?"

Jonathan stared for a long time at the wall, enjoying Lucy's exuberant delight as much as the thing itself. She was a different person when she was immersed in her own subject, and one of these days, she'd be just as enthusiastic about real life. He hoped he would be there to see it when it happened.

"I suppose those little hands at the ends of those lines are the blessings descending from Aton?"

Lucy nodded. "It doesn't seem bad enough to inspire such hatred, does it? Poor Akhenaton! A mere seeker after truth doesn't stand a chance when the realities of power are on the other side.

They could paint, though, couldn't they? They could write, too! You should read some of his hymns to Aton. They read just like the Psalms of David."

"It should make an interesting installment in the history of Egypt."

Lucy nodded. "One of the most interesting. Without Akhenaton's heresy we never really would have understood anything about Ancient Egypt."

They looked at the wall in silence for a while, each busy with his own thoughts. Neither wanted to exchange the moment for the glare of the sun and all that waited for them outside.

When Lucy got back to the hotel she found her room to be full of luggage. Faye emerged from the bathroom and sat down on the edge of one of the twin beds.

"Sebastian's here. He came back!" she announced jubilantly. "I said you'd give up your bed to him," Faye went on. "You don't mind do you?"

"Of course not." She could not help thinking that Sebastian had come in the nick of time.

Chapter Nine

"You're looking chirpy. Have you dealt with our little problem?"

Lucy turned and stared at her questioner. She liked Larry, finding him good at his job and ever ready to make things as easy for her as he could when he rigged his lights, often putting up the temperature by several degrees, so powerful were they.

"What little problem?"

"Oh, come on, sweetheart. We all know that Jonathan wants your sister out. Was it you who sent for the husband?"

Lucy eyed him blandly. "You all must know something that I don't. Faye and Jonathan get along very well together."

Larry chuckled. "Yes, and some of us have an eye as blind as a barn door, or whatever the expression is." He sobered quickly. "Is that what marriage to Miles Jameson did for you? Taught

142

you to look the other way whenever things got awkward?"

Lucy didn't deign to answer. "Did you follow Miles when he was racing?" she asked instead.

"Sure did. Everyone my age did. He was the only Briton around who looked as though he might win the championship. We all worshipped him!"

That was something Lucy had heard before—often. "Did you really all think he could do that well?" she asked curiously.

Larry looked apologetic. "His lifestyle came out only after he was killed. No one knew what he did off the racing track. He was a fool!"

"He thought he was living life to the fullest."

Larry smiled, his spirits restored. "He was still a fool. If you were my wife, I sure wouldn't have neglected you to paint some foreign town red. I'd have been at home with you where I belonged!"

"It was my fault, too," Lucy felt bound to tell him. "I hated the racing and it was his whole life. I wasn't the right wife for him."

"Perhaps not," Larry agreed. "He should have married your sister."

"Faye?"

"She'd have understood him better than you did."

"Men like her," Lucy conceded.

"In her place," Larry said, and deliberately winked at her. "With any luck she won't be bothering us today. I'd better get to work if I'm ever going to be ready in time. See you later, huh?"

Lucy stood and watched him go. He moved like a dancer, a handsome man who had a way with the opposite sex, and yet, as far as she was concerned, that vital ingredient was missing. How strange it was that one man could destroy one's defenses with a single look, while another could do no more than amuse. It had taken her a long time to learn the difference, she reminded herself. Between Miles and herself the chemistry had been lacking from the beginning and yet it was only now that she could admit it to herself.

"King Tut today, isn't it?"

The Irish cameramen were looking cheerful this morning, too. They knew all about the young King Tutankhamen; they'd seen the treasures that had been found in his grave.

"Hardly need a script conference on his tomb, do we?"

"You may not," Judy rebuked them. "It's a very enclosed space and I mean to get all the camera angles right, if you do not. Is Jonathan here?"

"We haven't seen him."

Judy turned to Lucy, lifting an eyebrow. "You must know where he is. I hear you were turned out of your own room last night."

"I found another."

"I thought Jonathan might have helped you out?"

"Then you thought wrong."

"The hotel's full," Judy went on, unwilling to relinquish a spicy bit of gossip.

"Is it?"

Judy flushed. "So I was told. I'd better go and find Jonathan if we're to get started on time. Have you all got your notes ready?"

They waved them at her, fanning themselves at the same time. It seemed hotter than ever and there wasn't so much as a breath of wind anywhere in the hotel. O'Reilly and O'Rourke made themselves busy arranging the chairs in a circle and ordering coffee while they waited.

"Are you sure you're not knowing where the great man is?" They grinned at Lucy.

"How should I know?" she answered.

She saw her sister and Sebastian coming out of the dining room and hoped against hope that they hadn't seen her. But at that moment, Sebastian turned his head and saw the little group in the foyer waiting for Jonathan.

"Have a good night?" he called out to Lucy. His smile could best be described as a leer.

"If anyone else asks me where I spent the night I'll publish the address on the notice board!" she announced crossly.

Sebastian put an arm round his wife's waist. He looked, Lucy thought, exactly like a red-headed rat. "Poor Lucy, you never have any luck, do you?" he said.

"Just what do you mean by that?" Lucy asked in a white rage.

"Yes, explain yourself," a deep male voice demanded. Lucy whirled around. It was Jonathan!

"I didn't mean anything," Sebastian blustered.

"No? Then why is the whole hotel alive with rumours that because you turned Lucy out of her room, paid for by the television company, incidentally, that she must have shared my bed?"

"There weren't any other rooms available."

"All the more incredible that you turned her out," Jonathan commented acidly.

"I think," Faye said on a giggle, "that Jonathan's accusing you of not being a gentleman, darling."

"Never pretended to be one!" Sebastian answered on a note of self-satisfaction. "At least I never married anyone under false pretenses."

"Not now, dear!"

Lucy looked at her brother-in-law's interested audience and groaned inwardly. If she didn't get rid of them, she'd never live it down with any of them.

"Hadn't we better get down to work?" she suggested.

"Not until Sebastian explains himself," Jonathan said pleasantly.

"Look, if it's about where I went last night—"

"It isn't. I want to hear about Miles."

"I don't!" Lucy exclaimed.

"You never did," Faye said dryly. "Miles might have told you if you'd been less determined to be the perfect little wife—"

"Told me what?"

"He couldn't have children; it was because of a children's disease. Mumps, I believe." It was Sebastian who spoke. Lucy knew he was enjoying himself. Like Miles had, he enjoyed humiliating those he bore a grudge against. His grudge against Lucy was the simple one that she earned more money than he did and he wouldn't have known about that if Miles hadn't openly boasted about it one day when they had all been together.

"Who said?" Lucy asked faintly.

"Oh, Lucy, the whole family knew! It was ages before we realised that Miles hadn't told you and it was too late then—you were married to him." Faye embraced her sister in apology. "Men! What was the point of telling you now?"

Lucy could feel the floor rocking under her feet.

"Then he knew we couldn't have children? He knew all the time?"

"You know Miles, love! He probably pretended it had never happened. Are you all right, Lucy? You look as pale as a ghost!"

"I've been hearing from one," Lucy said with a shaky laugh. "Why didn't anyone ever tell *me*?"

Faye looked increasingly distressed. She was

silly and thoughtless, but when she thought about her at all, she was genuinely fond of her sister.

"I would've told you if you'd ever decided to call it a day with him, wouldn't I, Seb? All you seemed to care about was making a name for yourself in a subject none of us could make head nor tail of. It seemed that Miles had a case against you, too."

"I thought you said I was busy being the perfect little wife?"

"You were at first. It would have been unkind to tell you then. I didn't want to spoil your happiness."

"Okay," said Lucy, "I can understand that. But when you knew I was far from happy, why didn't you tell me then?"

Faye looked uncomfortable. It was Sebastian who brazened it out. "There was no telling you anything then. University professors know everything anyway! I felt sorry for Miles when you turned into such a bluestocking. Dammit, what man wants his wife playing around with mummies when he wants her at home looking after him?"

"He wasn't at home very often," Lucy remarked.

"That could have been because you drove him away," Seb insisted defensively. "You would've driven me away quickly enough, let me tell you. You were never any fun! For weeks you never even laughed! I preferred Miles—except when he was making a pass at Faye. He could have anyone else, I told him, but a wise bird doesn't foul its own nest!"

Lucy had heard enough. She wasn't surprised that Miles should have tried his luck with her sister. She couldn't think of many females of their acquaintance with whom he hadn't. He had lied to her about it of course, he had lied as easily as he'd breathed. But it was the big lie she hadn't known, hadn't guessed even in her wildest dreams. His excuse had always been that she was less than a woman because she couldn't have children and therefore he had been forced to look elsewhere. Now the excuse was as threadbare as his morals had been and all she was left with was a distaste at having ever been associated with him.

Lucy didn't hear Jonathan swing into action. She paid no attention as he gave orders to Judy, hurried Faye and Sebastian out of the hotel, and came back for her.

"The others can run through the script without us," he said, taking her cold hands in his. "Is there anything in particular they should look out for?"

Lucy called the tomb up into her mind, glad to have something else to think about. "Only that we're not allowed to exclude the public entirely while we're filming, but Judy already knows that. We've already done the funeral furniture in the museum. I want to show some of the illustrations

on the wall and explain again a little about the
Book of the Dead. It was important for the
judgment of the soul to get everything right."

"Think you'll be ready to film this afternoon?"

Lucy tried to smile. "As ready as I'll ever be."

Oddly, it was one of the cameramen who
refused to go ahead with the filming that day.
"Guess we could all use a break," Paddy said.

They were all nice people, kind people, but
there was no way they could know what she had
been through with Miles. Perhaps it was just as
well. She didn't want to be seen as victim by
anyone. She'd spent years polishing her image in
quite another field. She particularly did not want
Jonathan to see her in that light. Her lips trem-
bled and she knew her cool, carefree facade was
about to crumble.

Jonathan bent his head and saluted her with his
lips on her cheek. "Forget it, my dear love. You
can get on with your own life now," he whispered.

The Valley of the Kings was baking hot. Jonathan stopped off at the concrete refreshment
building to get them a picnic for lunch. Lucy had
said nothing all the way over on the ferry and she
said nothing now, turning her eyes away in case he
should decide to say anything to her. The humiliation of the morning lingered in her memory.
Sympathy, from Jonathan was the last thing she
wanted. She didn't much care what any of the

others thought of her, but Jonathan's opinion meant more to her every day.

Jonathan came back to the car, wincing as he got in beside her. He piled the packets of food up on her lap with care, sliding a glance at her out of the corners of his eyes.

"Forget him—"

She spoke then, the words pouring out of her, almost out of her control. "Oh, for heaven's sake!" she cried. "I *have* forgotten him in every way that matters. He was eminently forgettable! You don't have to feel sorry for me!"

"Good."

The car jerked forward, almost sending her through the windshield. "Must you?" she complained.

"Something was needed to wake you up. And I'm not at all sorry for you. There isn't room for any pity of mine in that ocean of sympathy you have for yourself."

Was he right? Perhaps. Instantly she felt better. Smiling, she asked, "Where are we going?"

"Where would you like to go?"

The tomb of Tutankhamen wasn't far from the refreshment block. One could tell it from afar by the number of people milling about it. She wondered how Larry was getting on with erecting the lights.

Jonathan followed her glance. "No, not today. I'm up to here with Egyptology. I have other things on my mind right now. I've had a look round inside there already today. It took me half an hour to battle through all those characters trying to sell their junk to the tourists. It was that that made me late for the great denouement."

"It was meant to be a script conference."

He covered her hand with his own. "Have we got rid of your sister now?"

"I think so. Seb doesn't like Egypt. He'll take her back to England with him."

"And what about the lady love?"

"They never last long with Seb."

"No wonder you're turned off marriage! Where are we going?"

Lucy suggested the first place that came to her mind. "The Colossi of Memnon. I'm not turned off marriage," she added. "I prefer being a widow."

His glance slid over her before returning to the road ahead. "Where were you last night?" he asked.

It wasn't the question she'd been expecting. "Not you, too?" She groaned. "I went to another hotel. There *are* others in Luxor, you know."

"I've seen some of them. Why didn't you come to me? Most of those other hostelries are more suitable for men than for women."

"I managed," she said. She smiled with a touch of mischief, looking much more like her usual self. "Suleiman has a very large family. I need never lack for a bed in Egypt."

The Colossi of Memnon rose some twenty

metres above the plain. Jonathan drew up beside
them, a resigned look on his face.

"Okay, tell me about them before we have our
picnic," he invited her.

Lucy laughed. "All vandals aren't modern
ones," she began obediently. "These used to
guard the mortuary temple of Amenhotep III,
until Rameses II and his son carted the temple
away to use on their own building, leaving these
two behind. The Romans thought they were the
sons of the legendary Aurora, goddess of the
dawn. Memnon was a hero of the Trojan war who
fell at the hands of Achilles. End of story."

"Brief and to the point," he agreed. "It looks a
good site for a picnic."

It was cooler in the shadow of the gigantic
statues. Jonathan opened a couple of cans of
lemonade and handed one of them to her. It was
still cold enough to produce little droplets of
water on the outside. Lucy drank it very slowly,
savouring every sip of the ice-cold liquid. What
did Miles matter on a day like this? She would be
a fool to let him upset her life now, so long after
his death. What did anything about him matter
now?

"All our schedules are going to be thrown by
taking today off," she murmured.

"It was worth it to get Faye off your back. Why
do all your family think you're half-witted?"

"They won't admit that it's possible for a
woman to have goals in life of her own. It doesn't

matter how many successes one has, if one fails with the man in one's life, then one's a failure. My marriage with Miles was a ghastly failure long before he was killed, only none of us would admit it. Faye has at least held on to her man."

"If that's what it can be called," Jonathan said dryly. "Why don't you give her as good as you get?"

"Because I have something else and she hasn't. I don't normally see a great deal of her. She and Miles had quite a fling once and I couldn't feel the same about her after that."

"Is that what made you give up all thoughts of having another relationship with someone else?"

"There are worse things," Lucy said.

"Do you still feel the same way?"

Lucy nodded. "I think I do." She made an expansive, all-comprehensive gesture with her hands. "I'm going to be famous! That's enough for me for the time being."

While they had been talking some camels had strayed over to where they were sitting, grazing where there was nothing to graze.

Jonathan watched their awkward gait. "You know I used to know someone who walked as they do, thrusting out the same arm as leg," he said. "He was the least co-ordinated person I've ever met, but camels seem to manage quite well."

"They're beautiful! It gives them a lovely, swaying motion!" Lucy said.

"One of these days I'll have a camel race with

you across the desert. The loser will take the
winner out to dinner. How about that?"

"Sounds fair to me."

"When we've finished filming?"

"Won't you be going back to England?"

"Not immediately." That surprised her. "I
thought I'd stay on for a while and get to know the
country a little better."

"Wonderful! There's such a lot to see! I can
give you all the background information you'll
need. Not everything that's worth seeing is on the
usual tourist routes—"

"Stick around and be my guide," he suggested.

"Are you serious?"

"Never more so."

"What else would you expect?" she asked
suspiciously.

"This is your territory," he answered. "I'd let
you take the lead."

"I wouldn't go to bed with you, you realise
that?"

"We'll see."

"We won't see anything of the sort! I'm telling
you, Jonathan—"

"I'm listening, sweetheart. It's been a long,
hard few days. You may feel quite differently
when we're alone together and there's nothing to
distract you."

Earlier in the day, she would have taken of-
fence at that remark; now, she was merely amused. Nor was he so far wrong; she thought she

might very well end up accepting his offer. An affair with Jonathan would be much more exciting and rewarding than marriage to Miles had been.

"I've done with making a fool of myself over love," she informed him loftily.

"We'll be fools together!"

"I've grown too old for folly," Lucy said sadly.

Jonathan's eyes crinkled with amusement. "When did this happen?"

"This morning. I'm a slow learner or I would have learned my lesson long ago."

Jonathan moved in close before she was even aware that he had changed his position. She felt his hand on her shoulder and swung round to face him. Carefully he pushed her down onto her back, his head blotting out her view of both the camels and Colossi. The longing for his touch washed through her bloodstream leaving her weak with desire.

His kiss was possessive and expert, taking advantage of her uncertainty to gather her closer against him while he tasted the sweetness of her mouth with a thoroughness that left her in no doubt that he meant to be the master.

"I want to make love to you," he said. "I was going to give you time to decide you wanted me, too, but you see what you do to me. Lucy!"

There was little doubt that she wanted him, too. Her nipples hardened under his touch and she arched to meet the welcome weight of his body. There was a rightness about it she had never known with Miles and had never wanted to know with anyone else.

"Salaam elêkum!"

"We-'alêkum salaam!" Lucy responded without thought. The greeting penetrated her mind slowly and she pushed Jonathan away with a sudden energy that caught him unawares and sent him sprawling.

Two grinning faces swam into her line of vision. One of them was wearing what had once been a white Muslim cap.

"You are behind the rest of your people," he told her. "You and your husband will have to hurry to catch up with them."

"He isn't my husband," Lucy said.

The young man laughed down at her. "If he isn't your husband, he'd like to be," he suggested audaciously.

Jonathan threw back his head and laughed. "Have you come for your camels?" he asked the boy in English.

The boy squatted down onto his heels. "She says she isn't your wife," he began.

The other lad, more morose than his fellow, forbore to look directly at Lucy at all. He put in an occasional word as his brother asked what they were doing there, where they were from, and where they were going, and the most intimate details of their families.

"We must go," he said at last. "If you come to our village ask for us!"

"We will," Lucy promised.

"When you are married!" The boy said. With a final wave of his hand, he, his brother, and the camels were gone.

Chapter Ten

"Alone at last!" Jonathan said teasingly to Lucy.

"Mmm," said Lucy. It seemed a nice, safe reply that gave her time to think. Jonathan inched in closer to her.

"Shall we take advantage of it?"

"There'll be somebody else here in a minute."

"How d'you know?"

"This is Egypt."

Jonathan turned over on his back, shading his eyes with one arm. "What will it take to get Miles out of your system?" he asked after a time.

Lucy strove for honesty. "I've forgotten him in many ways. It was as much my fault as it was his that our marriage was a failure. I thought I was in love with him when all it was was a bad case of hero worship. Miles would never have married me for love. Hero worship was something he couldn't resist. He thrived on it. Unfortunately, mine for him died on our wedding night—"

"Clumsy brute!"

Lucy was silent for a long moment. "What makes you think it was his fault?" she asked at last.

He squinted at her through his fingers. "You forget that I've held you in my arms and kissed you. I know more about you, Lucy Jameson, than you know about yourself!"

"All that from so little?"

"Don't you believe me?"

"I'm not sure." She sighed. "I guess the chemistry wasn't right between Miles and me. Love doesn't have a lot to do with it, does it?"

"Sometimes."

She chewed on her lower lip. "It wouldn't have anything to do with you and me."

"Why don't you try it and see?"

She didn't know what she would have done if he had insisted. She stared at him, noticing all sorts of little things about him that she had been aware of before, but which now were as vivid to her and familiar as the sight of her own hands. She could shut her eyes and know exactly how the hair grew out of his scalp, and the way his smile was deeper on one side than the other.

"I think not," she said. "I need to get something sorted out for myself first."

"Okay, love, but don't take too long about it."

She was grateful that he made no move to touch her. If he had, she would have been lost, she knew. It made her heart pound just to think about it. She wanted to close the space between them and have him kiss her and hang the consequences! She gave him a speculative glance from beneath her lashes. She had never thought of herself having an affair with anyone, but then she hadn't known Jonathan before. Miles had wanted an affair. It had been she who had insisted on marriage. She wouldn't make the same mistake with Jonathan.

She turned over on her stomach, leaning up on her elbows, and began to doodle with her finger in the dust. When she was done, she was surprised to see she had made a cartouche out of Jonathan's name, such as those that were written out for kings, only she hadn't contented herself with only writing his name. Jonathan, my beloved, the one who brings happiness to my heart. She lifted a hand to wipe it away, to find her wrist grasped by Jonathan's fingers.

"Translate!" he commanded her.

"I was only playing."

His hand tightened on her wrist. "What have you written?"

She shrugged her shoulders. "Your name. When we first learned to read hieroglyphics, we all made cartouches of our names for fun. I was just trying out yours to see how it looked."

He reached for a small notebook in the pocket of his trousers and plonked it down in front of her, together with a ball-point pen.

"Write it down there!"

She took the pen from him. "Jonathan," she wrote, and enclosed it with a line.

He compared the two drawings, his eyes alight with interest. "This one has several additions," he pounced, pointing to the sand. "What do they mean?"

"They're artistic embellishments—"

"I like them. I'll have the lot in the one I can keep. Please, Lucy, write it again!"

Reluctantly she did so. What did it matter? she thought. It was unlikely that anyone else would ever translate it for him. Why should they? There were not many who could after all.

She drew the cartouche again: *Jonathan, my beloved, the one who brings happiness to my heart.*

She watched him tear off the bit of paper, fold it, and put it neatly away in his pocket. "Does it make you feel like a Pharoah, a King, a god in your own right?" she asked him.

"I'll let you know."

He leaned back, his eyes almost shut and with a lazy smile on his face. "What happened to Tutankhamen?" he asked her. "Was he murdered that he died so young?"

"Probably."

"It could be a dangerous business being Pharoah, then?"

Lucy nodded. "They think he was Akhenaton's brother. He was at a disadvantage from the start, having been a part of his brother's Great Heresy. He lost no time in going back to Thebes and restoring the old religion, but there were other eyes on his throne, men who could be relied on. I think they were always uncertain of poor Tut. He was probably done away with by his tutor Eye who married his young widow and ruled in his stead. King Tut was the last of the Eighteenth Dynasty. Things rather fell apart after him. Eye was superceded by General Harmhab and that was that. The end of an era."

Jonathan put out a hand, picking up hers and examining her fingers with close attention. "You've got a lot of knowledge stored away in that head of yours. Tell me what you keep stored in your heart?"

Lucy tried to take her hand away. "Nothing that would interest you."

"Tell me anyway."

She gave up the attempt to retrieve her hand. It was rather nice having it held. She took a deep breath. How easy it would be to fall in love with this man!

She leaned up, touching an explorative finger to where his collar touched his tan neck. "Would you believe that there have been a long line of tourists here before us?" There was a grain of sand between the material and his skin and she fished it out with her finger and spent a long time looking at it.

"There aren't many tourists here now," he said.

"They pass by in their charabancs now. Once, they used to come in their hundreds to test the truth of the myth that strange sounds came from the statues at dawn. Many of them wrote their names on the legs, as high up as they could reach."

Jonathan squinted to where she was pointing. "In Greek?" he queried.

"Some of them were Romans. If you read the inscriptions they'll tell you how the writers heard all sorts of things, just as they'd been told they would. Some heard a blast from a trumpet, some a musical note, and some of them voices chanting. Some of them even thought it was the voice of an angry god and were very much afraid."

Another grain of sand followed the first one. She hooked her finger deeper into his collar, exploring the hard muscles of his shoulder.

"What did they really hear?" he asked.

He was so still that she knew herself to be playing with fire.

"Some physicist came along and exploded the whole theory. It was nothing more than the contraction of the stone during the cool nights following the expansion during the heat of the day. It caused the splitting off of particles from the surface amongst other things. Worse than the physicists, however, were the repairs that were carried out in the time of Septimus Severus. They filled in all the holes and nothing was ever heard from the statues again."

"And the tourists fell away, I suppose?"

"We're the only ones right now," she pointed out.

The gleam in his eyes was distinctly unsettling. "I wondered if you'd noticed. What shall we do about it?"

"What would you like to do?" she inquired innocently.

She closed her eyes. "Mighty Aton, keep me safe!" she said inside her head.

"Hey, wake up there! What dreams are you dreaming now?"

"My dreams are my business!"

"Afraid of the light of day?" he taunted her.

She moved her head from side to side. "The sun knows me of old. How about you?"

His smile changed to a frown and she was sorry she had spoken. "I hadn't realised he'd followed you to Egypt!"

She winced. "He didn't. That isn't what I meant. I'd forgotten all about him, Jonathan. The only time Miles was up in the daytime was when he was racing."

She could have cried because the moment was gone. Miles was still able to reach out from the grave and ruin her happiness. Or had she done it to herself by not reaching out and grasping what was offered to her with both hands?

Jonathan cupped her face in his hand, forcing

her to look directly at him. "What do you want, little Lucy?"

She was silent for a long moment, every muscle braced.

"I want you," she finally said.

She would never forget the look on his face; the slight flush that had crept up from his neck; or the warm look in his eyes as he leaned over her.

"Say that again," he commanded.

"I want you," she repeated obediently.

"You can't say it too often for me! Even if I did have to force it out of you in the last resort."

"Really? I didn't notice." She was being deliberately provocative now. She had never thought it could be such fun to spar with danger like this. "Perhaps I wanted to hear a similar confession from you," she added, tongue in cheek.

"You've known I've wanted you from the first moment I saw you."

"I've never been lusted after before!"

"More likely you didn't notice." He sighed, a reserve slipping over his features that she found acutely depressing. "Miles has a lot to answer for."

"I can't blame Miles forever," she said.

He rolled away from her. Oh, Jonathan, she thought, I should never have made that prayer to Aton. I don't want to be saved from you at all!

"He was a clumsy oaf and better forgotten," he agreed. "I'm not sure I can be as gentle with you as you deserve. Come on, girl, we'll go back to the others before I do something we'll both regret."

"Not me!" She stayed exactly where she was, not moving a muscle. "I'll only think you don't want me if you don't kiss me now."

Jonathan came back to her, running his fingers through her black hair and pushing it away from her face, so he could study her. Finally, he asked, "Lucy, have you had other loves?"

She stirred in the prickly sand, suddenly aware of the rough pieces beneath her shoulders. Would it have been any better if she could have named a long list?

"I didn't want Miles to have any excuse to blame me for the failure of our marriage," she murmured. "Besides, he had reason enough already, I'm not sure I was cut out to be with a man—"

"Impossible! We're going to be beautiful together, beyond anything you ever imagined—"

Her eyes opened wide and there was no hiding the desire in them. "Now?"

He kissed her hard on the lips. It was a kiss of ownership, as if he were staking a claim to her that she wouldn't be able to deny ever after.

"No, not now." His voice was very gentle, almost a caress. "This isn't the time or the place. When I make love to you, darling, I don't want there to be any interruptions."

She bit her lip in disappointment. "I thought you wanted to have an affair with me."

He kissed her again. "Little fool, what do you know about affairs?"

"I have to know something. I am a widow after all."

"True, not that that proves a great deal in your case. My dear girl, no man has ever got near enough to you to matter to you. With me, it's going to be different. This is going to be an affair of the heart. Can you say as much of your marriage to Miles?"

"No," she admitted honestly. "But I thought it was. I wouldn't have married him if I hadn't. It took me a long, long time to find out I'd deceived myself as much as I'd been deceived by him."

Jonathan looked directly at her, standing with his hands on his hips. He reached down a hand and pulled her up onto her feet beside him. "It won't be like that with us," he said. "With us, it's going to be the sun, the moon, and the stars!"

"How can you be sure?"

"Because I never make a promise I can't keep."

Somehow, she believed him. She took a step closer to him, flinging her arms round his neck with an abandon that normally would have been foreign to her.

His kiss when it came was as soft as thistle-down. "Just keep on remembering that I'm not like Miles—not in anything! I want my woman by my side, not wandering round the world on her own!"

She made a face at him. "My job is important to me—"

"I know it is. You'll have to make up your mind which is more important, your work or the man in your life. You can have both, but not if your work is going to come first with you."

"It always has," she objected.

"Has it today?"

Today she had thought of nothing but him, but she was wise enough to know that it wouldn't always be like that. Tomorrow she would be back in front of the cameras and being a success on television was very important to her, too. She wanted to be a success in her own right, not just a racing driver's widow, and not in the shadow of any other man's existence.

"You don't understand, I love my job."

"Enough to be alone for months on end, while I wait for you at home?"

It sounded like a long-term affair if he was thinking of months, she thought. Months turned into years—

"Right now, I'd rather be with you, but it may not always be like that. You may want somebody else. *I* may want someone different—"

"If you do, I'll break your neck!"

His vehemence drove the breath out of her. She tried to turn away the tension of the moment with a joke. "You forget I'm going to be a star of the small screen! That could lead to anything!"

He smiled a lopsided smile. "Only with me as

producer and director, my dear. I intend to make sure of that. . . ."

When Lucy got to her hotel home she found a note pinned onto her pillow. The sheets were clean and starched, she observed. Probably by this time the whole hotel knew that Faye and Sebastian had taken possession of her room the night before. Everyone always knew everyone else's business in Egypt. It wouldn't have taken them long to have found out where she had gone to find a bed for herself. Probably even Suleiman knew about it by now. Suleiman's family always knew everything, often before one knew it oneself.

Lucy recognised the handwriting to be her sister's. She tore open the envelope with impatient fingers, not really wanting to read the contents.

"Dearest Lucy," she read. "We've gone back to England, as there was nothing for us to stay on for. Sebastian was afraid I'd fallen for Jonathan and is making the most of removing me from temptation's way. I wasn't able to find J to say good-bye to him. Just as well, as Sebastian makes me laugh when he plays the jealous husband.

"Don't allow Miles to spoil anything more for you. He never was worth all the misery he caused. Fun to be with for a short time, but not long-term. He would have been better off with me than a perfectionist like you! Love, Faye."

Lucy read the letter through twice, sitting on the end of the bed to read it the second time. She tried not to be glad they had gone. Her sister's marriage had always bored her, however. As far as she could see, there was no genuine emotion in it on either side. They both seemed to play any part that suited them at the time, changing roles as easily as they breathed. Well, at least now she wouldn't have to worry about Faye pursuing Jonathan. Lucy's mouth grew dry at the thought of her sister in Jonathan's arms, flirting with him as she had with so many others.

She crumpled Faye's letter into a little ball and threw it with a single, violent movement into the wastepaper basket. She had never felt anything approaching this about Miles. Miles had been a hero, he'd belonged to everyone, never really to her. That wouldn't do with Jonathan. She was in love with Jonathan and she was going to have him on any terms he offered.

Chapter Eleven

"Hey, Lucy, will you make a cartouche of my name like the one you made Jonathan?" Larry asked.

"If you like."

She was surprised that Jonathan should have shown the drawing she had done for him to anyone else. She was disappointed, too, because somehow she had thought that that was something between the two of them and not for anyone else's eyes.

She did her best with Larry's name, and then found herself having to do it for all the others. She was amused by their enthusiasm. They cavorted round like children, trying to find some of the symbols she had used on the walls of the tomb.

"I'm going to have mine made into a necklace," Judy told anyone who would listen. "I'll have it engraved on a tiny ingot of gold and wear it always. You're so clever, Lucy!"

Lucy denied it. It was easy to make short sentences once one knew what the symbols represented. She drew a few signs and put their equivalent sounds beside them. "See," she said, "it's easy!"

"What about numbers?" Larry asked her.

Lucy's face fell. She liked people to admire her Egyptians as she did. "Limited," she admitted. "There are signs for one, ten, one hundred, and one thousand, but they never invented anything for two through nine, so they had to write twelve as ten plus one plus one." There was no doubt that mathematics had not been the strongest point in the ancient world. Reluctantly, she went on, "Like the Romans, they never had a sign for zero. That had to wait for the Arabs sometime in the Middle Ages."

They all laughed and she knew they were laughing at her because she cared that the Ancient Egyptians had had their limitations.

"Why, it's well known," Jim O'Reilly said, "that the Ancient Egyptians were no more than the lost tribe of Israel on their way to Britain to become the British Israelites!"

Lucy sniffed. "I always knew the Irish would believe any fool thing one told them!" she retorted.

"You're jealous of our superior charm!"

"What charm?" she demanded.

Both cameramen pretended to be crestfallen. "Face it, Jim, she hasn't noticed it," Paddy said.

"As far as she's concerned we might as well not exist. The sun shines out of someone else entirely and we're left to break our hearts unseen and find what comfort we can elsewhere."

"Don't look at me, boys!" Judy smiled at them. "I have someone waiting for me back home."

"Women!" Jim grumbled good-naturedly. "They should never have been allowed to leave home and hearth and rush round the world unfettered, breaking hearts, holding out promises they can't possibly fulfill."

"Like what?" Lucy asked.

"Like sharing one of these gorgeous Egyptian sunsets over the desert with a lonely fellow like myself."

"Who promised you that?"

"It was a silent promise. I read it in your eyes and in your lilting smile, my darling."

"Huh!" said Lucy. "It shows you shouldn't judge by appearances—"

"I tell you, I read it in those darling, black eyes of yours. The pity of it was that it was for another man entirely. You'd have done better with my-self, there's no doubt about it, but then the female of the species was never known for her good sense, God bless her!"

"What good would a graceless Irishman be to us?" Judy asked. "We're otherwise catered for, thank you very much."

"Speak for yourself!" Paddy O'Rourke rebuked her. "A mummy doesn't do much for a girl."

"Mummies are a professional interest—" Lucy began with dignity.

"Miles Jameson is dead, too."

"There are other men in the world!" Lucy snapped at him. "And not all Irishmen either!"

The knowing looks made her blush. Fortunately the combination of the dark interior of the tomb coupled with her own gypsy looks meant that no one would have noticed. She would have recovered herself quite easily if Jonathan hadn't come down the passageway just then, his hair on the wild side and the frown on his face forbidding in the extreme.

"What's holding things up?" he rapped out at the assembled group.

"We're having a break before we go into the real thing," Judy told him.

"Anyone would think you want to be here all night," he grumbled, unappeased. "I told you Lucy needs an early night. It's been quite a day."

"Tomorrow is another day," Larry reminded him.

"I want to get this wrapped up tonight!"

"You're the boss," Larry said. "What's the hurry?"

Jonathan muttered something that none of them could hear. Lucy suspected they weren't intended to. If she could love him when he was as grumpy as a bear and feel nothing more than a strong desire to take him into her arms and soothe him down, she was well and truly hooked, she thought.

"Are you ready now?" Jonathan asked.

A clapperboard resounded through the eerie silence. Judy called out the sequence number in cool, measured tones. Taking a deep breath, Lucy began a slow walk through the tomb, talking as she went.

"What's this?"

She went on her way, concentrating on getting her timing right and not overloading her sentences as she was apt to do when she got excited about a particular point she was making.

"I said what's this? Who made these drawings?"

The scene came to a stop. Judy, normally the most patient of people, turned away from the prompter with an exasperated sound.

"Jonathan, what are you doing? You've ruined the whole take!"

"I want to know who made these drawings?"

"Lucy did!"

Lucy could feel his reproach from the corner where she was standing. "It didn't take long," she said. "They all wanted cartouches like the one I drew for you."

"So I see!"

The silence that followed his words was almost tangible.

Then Judy moved into the centre of the tomb, a smile pinned on her face. "I think we'll call it a day," she announced. "We'll film the rest starting at eight o'clock tomorrow morning. Please don't be late!"

The men gathered up their equipment and departed, grumbling under their breath as they went. Judy went after them, her shoulders unnaturally straight. None of them liked crossing Jonathan when he was in a bad mood.

"What was all that about?" Lucy asked when they were alone.

He shrugged his shoulders. "I'd taken my cartouche to be a personal love letter, not something to be spread around the whole crew."

"You shouldn't have shown them yours—"

He took the sheet of paper out of his pocket and spread it out on the sarcophagus in front of her. "I haven't shown it to anyone! Not to any member of the crew—"

"They all wanted one like yours."

"Devil take them! I thought they were all safely out of the way!"

"What for?" Lucy asked him.

"I wanted to know what you'd written."

"Oh," she said. "And did you find out?"

He bent over the cartouche, tracing the lines with the nail of his finger. "Yes, I did. Didn't you wonder why I was late for the filming?" He looked at her with increasing outrage. "You didn't miss me at all, did you?"

She put her head on one side, unwilling to give him the satisfaction of knowing how much.

"What did you find out?" she asked him.

His fingers ran over the cartouche again as she watched him. She wished they were touching her, more, she wanted his whole attention, to feel his arms about her and to know herself loved.

"He wouldn't translate it until you were standing beside me," Jonathan admitted. "What did you write, Lucy?"

So he didn't already know! "More than just your name," she said.

"I know that!"

"Who is this man who's going to translate it for you?"

"The man in the shop by the hotel."

Lucy's eyes opened wide in surprise. She knew the shop well and she liked the man who ran it, but somehow she had never seen him as a scholar.

"Abdullah! Now why didn't I think of that?"

He looked accusingly at her. "Are you laughing at me?" he demanded.

"Only a little bit. Do you mind?"

His eyes met hers as he shook his head. He held out his hand to her and she put her palm against his in a gesture of recognition. Slowly, she smiled at him, allowing him to pull her right up against him. Her mouth opened to his in silent acknowledgement of how right it felt to be in his arms again. The passion between them grew into a raging fire, only subsiding a little when he stepped away from her.

"We'll have to finish this somewhere else," he said. "We don't want to be locked in here all night."

"I wouldn't mind—with you."

He kissed her again. "Will you come to the shop with me?"

"If you like."

His fingers tightened in a small caress. "Have you succeeded in putting the past behind you? Have we a future together?"

She chuckled. "I think I may even enjoy it—one step at a time," she murmured, deliberately flirting with him. It wasn't a big thing, but it was the first time she had flirted with anyone for years. Miles hadn't enjoyed such innocent pleasures, and later on, she had been too afraid of exposing herself to hurt to take any risks.

His arm came round her waist and it did odd things to her breathing. Perhaps that hadn't been wise, she thought, for her timing was out of practice. She was absurdly nervous, though why she couldn't have said. It was time she grew up, she berated herself. More than time. If she couldn't be happy with Jonathan she wouldn't be happy with anyone.

He looked down at the hand he was holding. "I like your new confidence, but don't let it go to your head, my Lucy."

As they walked up the passageway and out into the open air, she knew she had made the right decision. She *trusted* Jonathan. He might not love her but he would be honest with her. She could depend on him in a way she couldn't even depend on herself. Too often in the past she had allowed hurt feelings to get the better of her judgment. That wouldn't happen with Jonathan. Jonathan had an integrity that nothing would change. How comfortable it was to know that.

She felt less comfortable on the ferry over to Luxor when he took out the cartouche and spread it out before her.

"Are you sure you wouldn't like to translate it yourself?"

For a moment she was tempted. She wanted to tell him that she loved him. She wanted him to know what he meant to her, why she was agreeing to having an affair with him when she had never thought of herself as other than the marrying kind. She wanted him to know that much about her because she trusted him not to take advantage of that kind of knowledge. He wasn't that kind of a man.

It came as a shock to her that she could at last admit that there were different kinds of men. There were plenty of men she had liked as friends, but as soon as there was any danger of them turning into lovers she had beaten a hasty retreat, seeing them all as the kind of monster Miles had been, or as unpleasant as she knew

Sebastian to be. Remembering without pain was a gift Jonathan had given her. Could she be equally generous? At least she could try.

"No," she said. "We'll have Abdullah translate it and then you can be sure I'm not making it up."

"You'd forgotten about him, hadn't you?" he accused her.

"I'm ashamed to say I had. With all you filmmakers about, I'd got to think of myself as the only expert around!"

"That won't do you any harm."

"It won't keep my secret either," she smiled at him.

He knew better than to make any public display of affection in a country where they frowned on such things. He made do with a squeeze of her hand and one of his tip-tilted, lopsided smiles.

"You don't have to jump through any hoops to please me, Lucy."

"I shan't mind," she said, and she meant it.

Nor was it as hard as she'd been afraid it might be. Abdullah greeted her kindly, brewing up some mint tea and keeping them amused by tales of all the tourist groups who had passed through recently.

"We had your professor here last month," he said to Lucy. "She spoke about you."

Lucy repeated her name with affection. "I didn't know she knew what I was doing," she said.

"Egyptian archeology's a small world and they

all pass this way sooner or later. She was glad you'd been chosen for this series, Mrs. Jameson. Of all her students she thought you were the one to interest the general public in her special love. I believe she wanted you to teach under her at one time?"

"Yes, she did," Lucy confirmed.

"Why didn't you?" Jonathan asked.

"I wanted to be a free agent for a while. It's hard to explain. It was a hard slog getting to where I am now—"

"And you don't want to give it all up, not even to teach?"

She shook her head. "I would if something better came along. Teaching was always something I knew I could do, but I prefer the rough and tumble of actually being in Egypt and working out here."

Abdullah poured her another cup of tea. She had long ago learned she would be expected to drink three cups of the tea to be polite, though the cups were so small that one could toss off the tiny amount of liquid involved in a single gulp.

"Being a TV star is better?" he inquired.

"It could be," Lucy said on a laugh. "If I ever become one I'll let you know."

"She's a natural," Jonathan told the other man. "After this one there are bound to be other series. She'll still be spending a lot of her time out here."

"With you?" Abdullah put in slyly.

"Possibly."

Jonathan got the cartouche out of his pocket. "I'm told you can translate this for me?" he said.

Abdullah took it from him. "Mrs. Jameson could do it better."

"My old professor would be better still," Lucy remarked, "but she isn't here." She was silent.

Abdullah looked from one to the other of them. "You won't?"

She shook her head.

Abdullah poured them both out their third cup of mint tea. "Your name, Jonathan, is written here," he said at last.

"Go on!" Lucy commanded.

Abdullah began painstakingly. "It says here, *Jonathan, the love of my life, my beloved.*"

"Right," said Lucy. She gave Jonathan a covert glance from beneath her lashes. He looked stunned. Anxiously, she searched for some kind of male triumph in the delight that was so apparent on his face. As far as she could see, there was none.

She took the cartouche from Abdullah, the laughter bubbling up inside her, and added a few more symbols underneath.

"There, tell him what that means!" she invited the Egyptian.

"Thou'rt bread and wine to my soul," Abdullah obediently translated, frowning over the paper. "Not very original, Mrs. Jameson!"

"No, it's not," she admitted. "I've always had a

thing about ancient Egyptian poetry though. One
of these days, when I'm rich and famous, I'll
translate a whole lot more and have them published. I'll dedicate them all to Jonathan."

Jonathan's fingers closed over hers so hard she
was afraid hers would break under the strain.

He stood up. "I'm taking Mrs. Jameson back to
the hotel," he announced. "Thanks, Abdullah,
for the tea and—everything."

"You're welcome!" The Egyptian grinned.
"Come back any time. I have many books you
and Mrs. Jameson may like to look through—"

"Some other time," Jonathan said.

Lucy said nothing at all. She shook hands with
Abdullah, half hiding behind Jonathan as she did
so. Part of her didn't want to leave the safety of
the shop; the rest of her couldn't wait to get away.
She wished he'd say something—anything—to
relieve the pressure of the moment. She had
declared herself with a vengeance and now it was
his turn. Supposing that wasn't what he wanted?
Did he want to take on such a responsibility? Yet
without him, her existence would be the pale gray
shadow that the ancients had considered death to
be. Not the Egyptians, she hastily amended to
herself, but the Greeks and the Romans. She
felt a sob in the back of her throat and concen-
trated hard on swallowing it. Not even the
Egyptians could compensate her for the loss of
Jonathan.

"Where are we going?" She tried to sound casual. Would he guess how insecure she felt?

He stopped in the middle of the street and looked at her. "Your room or mine?" he asked at length.

She swallowed again. "Is that wise?" she asked.

"Is there somewhere you'd rather go?"

"The Temple of Karnak."

She thought he was going to argue with her, but instead he summoned one of the horse-drawn carriages and helped her into it.

"You don't mind, do you?" she asked as he got in beside her. "Jonathan, I—"

"You don't have to say anything more, Lucy. It's my turn now."

His turn to say what? She had never been more nervous in her whole life. *Karnak*, she thought. What could she tell him about Karnak? Her mind was a blank. Her whole being was centred on the spot where his hand was lightly holding her round the waist.

She got out of the carriage as if in a dream, recognising the sphinx-lined avenue that led from the temple to the spot where the sacred barges had brought the god-king, Pharoah, to worship amongst his kin at the old capital, Thebes.

"Jonathan—"

"Don't say anything," he repeated. "Just take us somewhere where we can be alone."

She took him through the temple to a spot few

people knew about, where the herbs and medical instruments of so long ago had been recorded in stone by some unknown artist of long ago. The moonlight spilt over the massive columns and she thought she had never seen anywhere more beautiful.

"I love you, Jonathan," she said.

He pulled her into his arms with a hunger that warmed her and banished her nervousness as if it had never been.

"I know, darling. When are you going to marry me, Lucy?"

"Marry you?" she repeated, astonished.

"Isn't that what you want?"

"Oh, *yes*. But you, Jonathan, what do you want? I thought you wanted a brief affair—"

"I thought that was all you were willing to give me. I was prepared to accept any crumbs you offered me."

"Oh, Jonathan!" The wave of happiness that washed over her was almost more than she could bear. "Are you sure it's what you want?"

"That's what I was going to ask you!"

"Do you think I wouldn't want a lifetime with you?"

"I thought you might be a trifle daunted at the prospect. You did say one step at a time."

"That was for your sake. I thought, after a while, I might persuade you to love me a little?"

"You'll never know how much!"

She settled herself more comfortably in his

arms. For a while she couldn't say anything at all, she was too busy savouring the wonder of being loved by Jonathan. Then she said, "I love you, Jonathan. You're my first love and my last love. There never was another who—" She hesitated, at a loss to know how to explain it to him. In the end she went on in a few words of a strange language that even she had some difficulty in pronouncing.

"Translate, woman!" Jonathan demanded.

"Oh! thy voice is bewitching, beloved,
—This wound of my heart it makes whole.
Ah! when thou art coming, and thee I behold,
—Thou'rt bread and thou'rt wine to my soul."

She smiled up at him, rejoicing in his closeness, until the urgency of the moment took her beyond words, beyond anything she had ever known before, and there were only the two of them beneath the Egyptian moon.